"Let's call a truce."

David's gaze held hers in  aware we were at w

Addy refused to ba it's been a little...te

With a slight jerk of odd look. "Considering our past, how could it be anything else?"

"Can't we just be friends for a little while?" she asked in disgust. "We've only got a week to go. It wouldn't hurt to pretend to get along for your grandmother's sake."

"I suppose not. What would I have to do?"

"Well, for one thing, you could stop taking issue with everything I say." She opened her napkin with an audible snap. "Some men think I'm a fascinating conversationalist. A lot of them have found my company very enjoyable."

She watched his smile reappear as he gazed at her with lazy curiosity. "Really? How many?"

"If you're not going to take this seriously..."

He held up one hand. "Okay, trail boss. You win," he conceded, and tipped his beer bottle in a salute. "Bosom buddies from now on."

She cleared her throat and added primly, "Figuratively speaking."

His smile turned into a wolfish grin that made her shiver. "Of course."

Dear Reader,

Well, I guess you could say we have come to the final chapter. Nick, Matt and Rafe D'Angelo have all achieved their happy endings. Now it's Addy's turn.

I'm going to miss the entire family and Lightning River Lodge. I've had such fun creating these stories, and I hope you've enjoyed them, as well.

After three books set in and around the family lodge and the town of Broken Yoke, I wanted something a little different for Addy. Since she loves adventure and the lodge's stable, I thought it was time we explored a little of the area on horseback.

Now, I have a confession to make. I hate camping. When I was a kid, I didn't mind sand in my bed and mosquitoes in the tent. Okay, I did—but you just put up with it in those days. But now…my idea of roughing it is to stay in a hotel that doesn't have Internet access. I love fresh towels and room service. The idea that someone will not only bring food to you, but allow you to eat that meal in your pajamas if you want to is absolute bliss.

Thank you so much for allowing me to share these stories about the D'Angelo family. They feel like old friends to me, and I hope you feel the same way.

As Addy would say, Happy Trails!

Ann Evans

THE RETURN OF DAVID MCKAY

Ann Evans

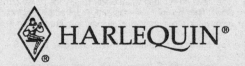

HARLEQUIN®

TORONTO • NEW YORK • LONDON
AMSTERDAM • PARIS • SYDNEY • HAMBURG
STOCKHOLM • ATHENS • TOKYO • MILAN • MADRID
PRAGUE • WARSAW • BUDAPEST • AUCKLAND

ISBN-13: 978-0-373-78115-7
ISBN-10:   0-373-78115-6

THE RETURN OF DAVID McKAY

www.eHarlequin.com

Printed in U.S.A.

ABOUT THE AUTHOR

Ann Evans has been writing since she was a teenager, but it wasn't until she joined Romance Writers of America that she actually sent anything to a publisher. Eventually, with the help of a very good critique group, she honed her skills and won a Golden Heart from Romance Writers of America for Best Short Contemporary Romance of 1989. Since then she's happy to have found a home at Harlequin Superromance.

A native Floridian, Ann enjoys traveling, hot fudge sundaes and collecting antique postcards. She loves hearing from readers and invites them to visit her Web site at www.Aboutannevans.com.

Books by Ann Evans

HARLEQUIN SUPERROMANCE

CHAPTER ONE

SURROUNDED BY CHINTZ and needlepoint, David McKay stood in the middle of his grandmother's living room and spread his hands in desperation. Somehow, he just had to get through to her.

"Please," he said. "I'm begging you for the last time. Don't do this."

Geneva McKay exhaled a little sigh. She folded another blouse into the tapestry carpetbag that sat open on the sofa. "I'm sorry, David. I've listened for almost an hour now, and this discussion is becoming quite tiresome. Really, dear, you shouldn't have flown out here."

At just a tad over five feet two, Gran might be dwarfed in his presence, but David knew she was hardly intimidated. He was—as she liked to put it—a big-shot Hollywood producer in an expensive suit, but she'd always see him as her little boy, eating mud sandwiches in the backyard and kissing the dog on the lips.

Since his arrival in Broken Yoke this morning he'd been relentless in his arguments, but nothing he said seemed to make any difference. Her mind was made up. Probably had been from the day her darling Herbert—David's grandfather—had breathed his last. In her words, only that silly problem with her heart last year had kept her from carrying out his wishes. Stubborn old woman.

"This is insane!"

"Don't be impolite," she admonished without glancing his way. "It's not insane at all. My friend Shirley says it's carmel."

"That's *karma,* and it's no such thing." David raked a distracted hand through his hair, hair he'd paid a fortune to have groomed on Rodeo Drive yesterday. He frowned and gave his grandmother a probing look. "Isn't Shirley the one who thinks aliens are trying to contact her through her toaster?"

"Not since she sold it in a garage sale."

He pressed his lips together and begged ethereal gods for patience. "Gran, if you're absolutely set on doing this, let me charter a plane. We'll fly to this Devil's Smile area and you can scatter Grampa Herb's ashes all across the state of Colorado if that's what you want."

"Oh, that's just like you, David. So practical. And unsentimental." She shook her head regretfully. "But I'm afraid it just won't do. I've waited far too long as it is."

She walked over to the fireplace, where, in an oddly ornate carved box, her husband's ashes held a place of reverence on the mantelpiece. Lovingly her fingers drifted across the sealed lid.

"Two years poor Herbert's been sitting here, and every time I look at this box I remember his last request. Don't you?" She sighed wistfully, and her pale blue eyes lost their focus as she revisited old memories. "'Gennie,' he said, 'those two weeks of our honeymoon were the most precious days of my life. Don't file my ashes away in some vault like a forgotten library book. Take me to the Devil's Smile.'" She straightened her thin shoulders. "So I'm going back to that canyon. And don't take this the wrong way, David, but you can't stop me."

Thoroughly frustrated, David moved to capture his grandmother's slim body between his hands. He didn't have time for this. There were already meetings long overdue and more to be scheduled. How could one old woman be so hardheaded?

He let his features settle into creases of concern. "Physically you're in no condition to do this."

"Oh, pish. I'm not decrepit, you know. Miranda Calloway went white-water rafting with her family, and she's seventy-six. Three years older than I am."

"Miranda Calloway didn't have heart surgery, did she?"

She gave him a perky smile, satisfied as a robin who'd just spied a fat worm in the grass. "No. So you see, I'm in better shape than she is. Do you think there'll be room on the pack mule for my sketch pad?"

"A week on horseback to get into the canyon. A week to get out. Sleeping in a tent on the ground. This won't be easy."

"I'll be fine. Before Herbert retired and we moved here, we traveled all the time. We were pioneers. Why, when we lived in Arizona, wild Indians were still a threat."

"Pioneers!" Incredulity escaped David in a short laugh. "Gran, you lived in a three-bedroom tract home in the suburbs. And if the Indians were hostile, it's because you probably cheated at reservation bingo."

His grandmother placed her hands on her hips to give him a scalding gaze he remembered well from childhood. "You're being quite impertinent, young man. It's that dreadful Hollywood influence. You never used to be so disrespectful when you lived here."

David thought he was pretty tough. So how could this old lady manage to scissor him up in ten seconds flat without mussing a single white hair on her head?

"I apologize," he muttered. Then he added, "I'm just worried about you. I love you, Gran."

Her eyes full of love, she touched a wrinkled hand to his cheek. "Oh, David. You really are a sweet boy. Always have been. I remember when—"

"Don't change the subject. This tour

company that's taking you out to the Devil's Smile—have you at least checked them out?"

Geneva waved away that concern with a ruffle of bony fingers. "That wasn't necessary." Returning to the sofa, she held a pair of flowered golfing shorts against her reed-thin body. "Do you think these are too busy? I don't want to look like a tourist."

"My God, you don't even know if this company is reputable? I can just see some tobacco-spitting cowpoke dragging you out into the middle of nowhere, stealing your purse and then leaving you in a cloud of dust."

"Don't be silly," his grandmother replied with an absent frown. "Why would I take a purse on a camping trip?"

David's teeth were starting to ache from being ground together. "What do you know about them?"

"Everything I need to. I'll be in excellent hands."

Before he could say anything more, their dispute was interrupted by the sound of the doorbell, followed by a playful knock.

She seemed momentarily flustered. "Oh, dear. Right on time, and I'm not ready yet."

She hurried to the door, and with a disgruntled groan David turned away to look out the wide front window. He couldn't see much of the driveway, just the tail end of a white van. No logo from what he could tell. Not much of a recommendation.

Gran opened the front door wider. David glanced over his shoulder, prepared to dislike what he saw.

He'd expected a man, but it was a woman who came into the house. She wore tight jeans and had legs that went on forever, almost a dancer's body. As she took off her Stetson, a cascade of black hair swung free to slide across her shoulders and glint in the sunlight.

"Good morning," the woman said in a bright, sweet voice. "Isn't this a great day to start an adventure?"

David's mouth parted in surprise.

This was no stranger who'd come to cart his seventy-three-year-old grandmother out into the wilderness. He knew this woman. Intimately. Or at least he had ten years ago.

The woman chatting with Gran in the foyer was Adriana D'Angelo.

Addy.

His first love from high school. The woman he might have married once upon a time. Until they'd both discovered that they wanted very different things out of life. Until she'd accused him of being willing to do anything to make his way to the top.

He felt a stirring of interest zip through his veins. He hadn't seen her since they'd had their last argument at Lightning Lake up at her parents' resort. Even though he'd occasionally come back to Broken Yoke to see his grandparents, to help out his grandmother after his grandfather had passed away, he'd managed pretty successfully to steer clear of Addy.

But now here she was, about to get as big a surprise as he had.

Why hadn't Gran said anything about Addy being involved? She'd known their bust-up had been acrimonious. Had she intentionally kept it a secret?

Before he could decide, Addy followed his grandmother into the living room. He moved out of the shadows and into the center of the room, determined to put up a good front.

She'd been smiling at something Gran had said—and then she saw him. That smile froze in an expression of shock that he knew must be the mirror image of his.

"David?" she said, stopping dead in her tracks. She stared at him hard. He met her eyes with an impact that was like a head-on collision.

"Hello, Addy."

He couldn't get out more than that. Some damned malfunction in his throat. All the harsh words between them were as fresh in his brain as today's news. So was the way it felt to hold her, how her lips tasted. The memory of firelight on her skin.

Funny how you could fool yourself. Go ahead, climb the greasy pole of success. Make money hand over fist. Take risks and turn people's lives inside out. It could still come down to this. One look, and whatever your life had been before was up for grabs.

As though aware of the uncomfortable silence, Addy found her voice. "What are you doing here?" she asked.

Was there a trace of annoyance in her tone? He wasn't sure, but he felt irritated enough to harden his response a little. He lifted his brow. "What? I'm not allowed to visit my grandmother?"

"Well, you hardly ever do." The words must have come out with more feeling than she'd wanted, because he watched color crawl up her neck. "I mean, what are you doing here right now? Geneva and I are heading out on a two-week camping trip starting tomorrow."

"Not if I have anything to say about it."

"Oh, don't listen to him, Addy," Gran said with a dismissing wave of her hand. Turning to him, she added in a pained voice, "David, dear—"

He'd finally had enough. "Don't 'David, dear' me. It was one thing to think of you taking off in the company of some grizzled cowpoke, but there's no way you're trotting off into the Colorado wilderness just the two of you. I forbid it."

His grandmother stiffened. "David!" she snapped. "You're being unforgivably rude. You can't forbid me to do anything. We're perfectly capable of—"

"Excuse me, may I say something?" Addy interceded. She gave David a mild look of understanding that only made him suspicious. He watched her with bright, mistrustful eyes, like a caged hawk. Addy had always had her share of persuasive talents, too. "David, I doubt if we can communicate without it getting…unpleasant. But, really, this isn't about you or me. It's about what your grandmother wants to do."

"What she wants is unthinkable for a woman her age."

"I understand your concern. Initially I had some reservations myself. But your grandmother is perfectly aware of the demands of this trip."

"I certainly am," Gran cut in. "David, I love camping out. Remember the safari your grandfather and I took to Africa the year before he died? This will be a walk in the park."

Addy turned toward him again. "According to her doctor, she's in excellent health. And, frankly, her mind is made up. Unless you know of some *mental* impairment that would make her incapable…." She looked at him, all innocence. "Do you?"

Gran sniffed indignantly. "He most certainly does not."

David's patience had never been limitless and it was failing him miserably now. He glared at Addy. He couldn't help noticing that she still had eyes like those in a Vermeer painting, untroubled and frank. At the moment there was just a touch of amused superiority in them. She had him. He couldn't hurt Gran's feelings with an insinuation that she might not be fully capable of making this decision.

Sullenly he said, "It's nothing like that and you know it."

Satisfied, Gran turned back to her carpetbag and tugged the two sides together. Wordlessly David pushed her hands gently aside to complete the task for her.

He glanced back at Addy. "How many times have you made this trip?" he asked.

"Not counting this one?"

"Yes."

"None. But you know I've ridden all my life. We've recently added trail rides to the lodge's list of amenities, so I'm getting more and more experience taking tours into backcountry. Three just this month. I've never packed in as far as the Devil's Smile before, but I think I can get us there and back without falling down a prairie-dog hole. Is that good enough for you?"

"Of course it is, Addy," Gran answered for David. "I think I'm all set, so we can just be on our way." She patted David's hand. "Now give me a kiss, dear, and scoot back to Hollywood. I promise to call you as soon as I return."

"Gran—"

His grandmother clasped her hands to her face. "Oh, dear, I nearly forgot Herbert. Wouldn't that have been silly?"

She hurried to the mantel, then returned with the ornate box clutched tightly against her breast. In no time, Grampa Herb's ashes were efficiently stowed in the same zippered compartment as Gran's toiletries and sketchbook.

David was aware of Addy waiting patiently with a casual remoteness. The sunlight pouring in the front window gave her features a pretty glow, and the fact that he'd noticed at all annoyed him even further.

When his grandmother reached out to grab

the handle of the carpetbag, he let his larger hand settle over hers. "Gran—"

She straightened, her face flushed with determined irritation. Gran had a will no ax could break, and her tolerance was at an end. "David, I mean it now. There's nothing left to say."

There was a moment's pause in the struggle between them, like two combatants testing their weapons. Right now his armor felt pitifully inadequate. "I only have one thing to say," he tossed out.

Gran sighed wearily. "What's that, dear?"

"I'm going with you."

"What?" Both women spoke at once.

"I'm going on this trip with you."

Gran shook her head. "You can't do that."

"Why not? You said you don't leave until tomorrow morning. I assume you're staying up at Lightning River Lodge tonight. I'll throw some things together and meet you up there."

"Sorry," Addy said quickly. "We're booked solid."

Her response came too quickly for him to believe it. Besides, he wasn't going to let that weak attempt to outmaneuver him get in the way. He shrugged. "Then I'll stay here tonight and come up tomorrow."

"But what about your work?" his grandmother asked. "Don't you have—I don't know—wheeling and dealing to do? Worlds to conquer?"

"World conquering is slated for next month. In the meantime, I have enough capable people on my staff to take care of things while I'm away." He turned toward Addy. "Can you provide an extra horse or do I have to bring my own?"

He knew by the shifting of her eyes that she wasn't pleased, but she managed to answer in a clear, indifferent tone. "I can fix you up with a mount and pack mule. Do you still know one end of a horse from the other?"

"Mount from the left. Giddyap. Whoa." He shrugged. "What more do I need to remember?"

"I won't have one of our animals ruined just so you can win this argument."

Now that the decision was made, David was beginning to warm to the idea. He grinned. "I'm kidding. Just like riding a bike.

You don't forget. And didn't we ride all the time when I lived here before?"

He knew instantly those words were a mistake. Any reminder of their shared past would be sticky.

As though sensing that the sudden silence needed to be broken, his grandmother spoke up. "Dearest, it would please me immensely to have you come along, but you know how you get…."

"What's that supposed to mean?"

"Well, you like things…tidy. And you're always complaining about hotels that don't have decent room service or a health spa where you can work out. And don't forget that unfortunate garter snake incident."

"For God's sake, Gran," David said in a tone full of stung pride. "I was just a kid. And I think I'm capable of putting up with a few inconveniences. Remember *Sahara Sunset* last year? We filmed for three straight months in the desert, and I did just fine."

Addy crossed her arms over her breasts and narrowed her eyes at him. "You were on the movie set for three straight months?"

She probably knew damned well it wasn't

true. Producers didn't have to hand-hold every production they oversaw, and David had been lucky to do most of the work on that film long-distance. Come to think of it, maybe that was why the thing hadn't had big box-office success. But that was beside the point.

He gave Addy a sharpened look. "I *know* how to handle myself. Do you have any *legitimate* objections to my going?"

"You mean other than the obvious one? That we really don't…get along?"

Boy, talk about an understatement, he thought. But what he said was, "Yeah. Besides that."

She shrugged. "Not if you can keep up. I'm not a babysitter."

"I'll manage."

"Great. I can always make use of someone to pound tent stakes and carry water."

He realized that he'd missed her habit of coming back at him with mockery and sarcasm. Addy had always been able to give as good as she got. The next two weeks spent in her company might be very irritating…but strangely stimulating.

She rifled through a small stack of papers that poked haphazardly out of the notebook she carried, then handed him a brochure and a supply list. "Think you can pull it together on such short notice and find your way to the lodge? I want to leave at sunup."

"No problem. I'll be there."

Seeming resigned to the idea, she hefted one of his grandmother's bags and left him to get everything else. While his grandmother locked up the house, the two of them settled the luggage into the back of the lodge van.

"Oh," Addy remarked as though she'd just remembered something. She slammed the vehicle's tailgate, then moved closer to him so that her words wouldn't carry. "Two things I think we should get clear between us right up front."

He waited.

Her dark eyes had such a fearless, challenging look in them, a look he vividly remembered. How little she'd changed over the years. "This all might be an amusing lark to you, but this kind of trip is serious business. That means out there, what I say goes."

"You're the trail boss, huh?"

"That's right," she agreed. "Fail to pull your own weight or treat me like some flunky out of your corporate steno pool, and I'll have you hitchhiking back to the ranch in thirty seconds flat." Her eyebrows lifted. "Get the picture?"

"I think so."

"Good."

With that, she started to walk away. David stood back from the vehicle. He supposed he ought to be annoyed. But, oddly enough, he wasn't. Instead his heart was beating with newfound interest. He felt as though he had drunk some of the strong, glowing sunshine all around him.

"Addy," he called.

She turned to look at him, waiting.

"You said *two* things. What's the second one?"

She smiled, this time without the stiletto in it. "This trip is important to your grandmother," she said softly. "Don't spoil it for her. I'm going to have a couple of mules to keep in line. I don't need a jackass, as well."

CHAPTER TWO

TWO WEEKS WITH DAVID McKay back in her life.

Two whole weeks.

Oh Lord, how was she going to handle that?

All the way up the mountain road to Lightning River Lodge that question circled in Addy's brain. Unfortunately no answer ever circled with it.

Ten years had passed since she'd last seen David. Ten years since they'd argued past the point of all good sense. And now he was back. Back in Broken Yoke, a place he supposedly hated, surrounded by the trappings of a life he'd been eager to ditch. Soon to be spending day after day in the company of a woman he'd once accused of trying to stifle his creativity and tie him down.

Two weeks was going to seem like an eternity.

The interior of the van was quiet for so long that Geneva cleared her throat and looked over at her sympathetically. "I'm so sorry about the way this has turned out, Addy. I know having David along will make you uncomfortable."

"No, it will be fine," she said quickly and wished she meant it. "We're both adults. It was a shock at first, seeing him again, but we'll manage."

"I can't believe he's coming with us, but you know how he is when he gets an idea in his head. So…unstoppable."

"Oh, yes. I remember."

She did, too. She'd known him since the seventh grade, when he'd come to live with his grandparents. But it was the summer after high school had ended that she remembered most.

He'd told her that he'd been hired to do grunt work for the film crew that had come to Broken Yoke. *Trailblazer* had been a low-budget Western shooting in the nearby Arapahoe National Forest. From the time

David's father had given him his first camera as a child, he'd wanted to be a filmmaker. This had been his big chance to see what it was like from the inside.

She should have known right then that things were going to change for them.

From the corner of her eye Addy saw Geneva shake her head. "I had no idea he was coming home. He seldom does, you know."

"When was the last time?"

"When he helped me settle Herbert's estate two years ago. Since then I've been out to see him in California, of course, but I don't like it much. All that endless sunshine and plastic-looking people everywhere. It's just not right."

"I guess he likes it."

"I suppose," Geneva said in a clearly mystified voice. After a while she added, "I never dreamed he'd show up on my doorstep. I wish I could have warned you somehow. But it happened so fast." She reached across the seat and placed her hand on Addy's. "Are you sure you're going to be able to handle this, dear?"

Addy wished Geneva would stop asking

her that. Especially since she didn't know the answer. All she could say was, "As long as he earns his keep on this trip. No free rides."

"I'm sure he will. And you're right. It will be fine. You two got along so well in the old days, before he decided to go back to Hollywood with those wretched film people. It would be nice if you could be friends again."

Addy stole a glance off the road to look at Geneva. Had there been some wishful thinking going on in that head of hers? Surely not. But just to be safe, Addy thought she'd better nip that in the bud. "Not likely. We're two very different people now. Did you see that suit he was wearing? I'll bet he doesn't know what it's like to walk among us common folk anymore."

"I suppose we'll just have to wait and see what the next two weeks bring," Geneva said with a bright smile.

Addy took the last familiar turn toward home, and in no time they were in front of Lightning River Lodge. The sky at dusk, all shadows and light blended to perfection, gave the resort's wood-and-glass architecture a powerful, glowing presence among the tall pines. Beyond the lodge, Lightning Lake sparkled with late sunlight as though it were dressed in salmon-colored sequins. In the distance, the mountains sat like silent sentinels. It was a sight Addy never tired of.

Geneva McKay sighed. "Oh, it's so peaceful up here. I can't wait to spend a little time with your family before we leave tomorrow."

The lodge—sixteen rooms and two suites—had been built years ago by Addy's mother and father, Rose and Sam D'Angelo. They'd raised three sons and one daughter in the private quarters behind the downstairs lobby, and Addy had never known any other home.

"You haven't been up here since Mom's birthday party, have you?"

"No. And I'll be interested to see where my painting ended up."

A while back, Addy's father had commissioned Geneva to paint a portrait of her mom. A talented artist in her younger years, Geneva now had her work in a place of honor over the family's living room fireplace.

"There was a lengthy conversation about

where it should go, but Pop won. They'll be so glad to see you. And, frankly, your being there will take a little of the heat off me. Things have been a little…testy…between me and Pop lately."

Geneva gave her a knowing look and reached over to pat her hand. "I heard."

"Who told?"

"Your mother. She said she's really all right with whatever you decide, but she'd like to wring your father's neck."

Addy couldn't help but laugh. She felt exactly the same way.

A couple of weeks ago, Addy had come to a life-changing decision, and once she'd told the family, it had been like being in the middle of a presidential debate. The D'Angelos loved a good, loud discussion, and no one ever kept their opinions to themselves.

But you'd think a topic as sensitive as artificial insemination would have left them speechless for at least a day or two.

It hadn't. While most of the family had seemed stunned but openly supportive when Addy announced that she was interested in finding out more about the procedure, Pop had been furious. What was wrong with having a baby the old-fashioned way? Through love and marriage?

Addy had patiently explained to him that the man of her dreams didn't seem to know where she lived and that she wasn't getting any younger. Then the fireworks had started. Truthfully this trip out to the Devil's Smile would be a nice break from all the recent tension in the household.

Stopping under the front portico, Addy signaled to George, the front desk clerk and bellman, that she needed help with luggage. As he collected Geneva's bags, Addy said, "I've put you in one of the ground-floor rooms so you won't have to battle the stairs. Pop still refuses to put in an elevator."

Sam D'Angelo had suffered a stroke a couple of years ago, and though he was reliant on metal crutches occasionally, he refused to make many concessions for his health. Even Nick had given up trying to convince him.

"The parking lot is so full," Geneva said, glancing around.

"We're pretty busy this week. Mom and

Pop might put you to work if you're not careful."

"So what do you do every day, dear?"

"Anything that needs doing," she replied.

That was true. After college, she had fallen into her parents' expectation of joining the family business. Pop was still the head of the household and oversaw the bottom line. Mom ran the kitchen like a field marshal. Aunt Renata took care of the dining room, and Aunt Sofia kept the rooms shipshape. Her oldest brother, Nick, once a Navy pilot, ran helicopter tours from the resort in his two R44 Ravens. And though brothers Matt and Rafe lived down the mountain in Broken Yoke, they were often here with their wives, helping out when circumstances called for it.

As for Addy, professionally she was still finding her niche. She had her pilot's license so she could help out Nick when tours backed up, but she couldn't honestly say she loved it. Cooking bored her. As for the book-keeping she'd been relegated to lately by her father…well, as Nick diplomatically claimed, she had no flair for numbers.

She loved kids and she was good with her nieces and nephew. Maybe that's why it had seemed so sensible to stop waiting on Mr. Right and just do something about it….

She got Geneva settled in her room, then hurried off to help her mother in the kitchen. There were three special occasions planned in the dining room tonight—the wedding anniversary of a couple who'd met at the lodge twenty-five years ago and two birthday celebrations. They required extensive preparation and every available hand.

When she entered the kitchen, the first person she saw was her sister-in-law Dani, who'd married Addy's brother Rafe two months ago. Evidently the night was going to be busy enough that reinforcements had been called in.

Dani was seated at the big butcher-block table, trying valiantly to carve radishes into roses for garnish. She wasn't doing a very good job of it. As soon as Dani saw Addy, she beckoned her over with her paring knife. Addy snatched up an apron and gloves, putting them on as she came to Dani's side like a doctor approaching a patient on the operating table.

"Save me," her sister-in-law begged in a low voice. "Both your mother and Aunt Ren have shown me how to make these darned things, and I still don't know what the heck I'm doing."

Addy lifted a radish and squinted at it. It resembled a pinecone more than a rose. "Gee, it doesn't show."

She removed the knife from Dani's hands. "Go see what help Aunt Ren can use. I'll take care of these."

Dani was the newest addition to the D'Angelo clan. Although she was a newspaper columnist by profession, so far she didn't seem to mind the way a person could get sucked into the family business at a moment's notice.

Addy liked her a lot. Growing up, she had been closest to her brother Rafe, once the wild child in the family. She was glad that he'd settled down at last, that he'd finally found a reason to come home and a woman worthy of coming home to.

She picked up a radish and began making the cuts that would turn it into a flower. Carrot curls. Tomato stars. Even squash swans. She knew how to make them all. A Jill-of-all-trades.

And absolutely a master at nothing.

ONCE THE DINING ROOM closed, things settled down at the lodge quickly. Guests usually kept early hours because of all the daytime activities the area offered, and tomorrow promised to be a beautiful day just made for outdoor fun.

With one person manning the front desk after hours, the family often sat around the living room of their private quarters, drinking coffee or sharing a bottle of wine as they compared notes about the day. Tonight Geneva McKay had been invited to sit with them. Although she was some years older than either Rose or Sam, they had all known one another for years.

Addy sat in a back corner, listening to the conversation with one ear. She was tired, and for some reason her nerves felt jangled. She supposed it was just anticipation of the trip, the go-go-go of this evening's workload. And the fact that it seemed as though every few minutes someone mentioned David's name.

She didn't think it was intentional, but she found it unsettling. It was only natural that her father or mother would ask Geneva about David, but it didn't end at that. Didn't they remember that Addy was his ex-girlfriend? Didn't they care about her feelings at all?

While it was nice not to have to field questions about her future baby plans, Addy didn't want to hear about how successful David had become. How he owned a condo in New York and a flat in London and a beach house in Malibu. She didn't need to know whom he'd escorted to the Oscars last year and how he'd met the Queen when his last big blockbuster had premiered in England.

Besides, Addy already knew most of it anyway. Over the years she couldn't help following his career with some interest. A handsome, rich, powerful man like David McKay—the boy wonder of Hollywood—made the news often.

Addy rubbed her temple to soothe away the headache she felt behind her eyes. At her father's urging, Geneva was telling how David had recently taken up hang gliding. How his instructor said he was a natural at it.

"There's almost nothing that boy can't do," Geneva said, a proud note in her voice.

"Really?" Addy asked suddenly, feeling perverse. "Can he walk on water yet?"

Amazing how quiet a room could get. It seemed as though everyone turned to look at her. Even Rafe, who'd been stealing kisses from his wife on the couch.

Geneva seemed puzzled, but it was her father who spoke. "Adriana," Sam said, "is something bothering you?"

Addy felt immediately contrite, the coffee turning to acid in her throat. This definitely wasn't like her. "I'm sorry, Geneva," she said quickly. "That was uncalled-for."

"It's all right, dear. I do tend to go on a bit about David when I have a captive audience."

Addy stood. "I have a headache, and it makes me poor company, I'm afraid. Will you excuse me? I need to check on a few things for our trip. Good night, everyone."

She sailed out of the room before anything more could be said. With self-conscious haste, she went through the lodge and out the front door into the night air, heading for the barn.

The moon made pearly ripples on Lightning Lake as a breeze sifted through the trees. Although quite beautiful, tonight she had no interest in it. *Not there,* she thought. *Definitely not there.* The lake held too many memories of her time with David. Those last bitter words between them.

She just wanted to be away from people right now. Just find some way to…to *shut down* for a little while. To stop thinking.

The barn offered that kind of release. It sat in a clearing, surrounded by white-trunked aspens. It wasn't huge, just eight stalls with a small corral attached, but as she slipped the latch and flipped on the light, her breathing calmed a little.

She loved the family business, but she felt especially passionate about the stables. Addy had finally convinced her father that they needed to reopen the old barn. Trail rides and overnight camping trips had been added to the list of amenities, and Addy enjoyed being responsible for this new enterprise. She loved the people she met, the animals she tended as though they were her own children.

Children. Could she manage this part of the business *and* take on the challenge of single motherhood? Of course she could. Women juggled a career and home all the time these days.

And there was always Plan B. If she needed help during or after her pregnancy, she could call on Brandon O'Dell, the lodge's front desk manager. He'd been a friend of Nick's for years, and he and Addy had dated briefly. Last week he'd shocked her, asking flat out if she was interested in becoming a partner both professionally and personally.

Marriage to Brandon—whom she didn't love but whom she might grow to—or raising a child alone. *That* decision hadn't been made yet.

Either way, would it be enough to keep her from being envious of her brothers? Nick, Matt and Rafe had all built lives of their own. They had wives and children and homes where she felt certain they lived in a harmony and love that seemed to have bypassed her entirely.

What had she been doing wrong? Why

hadn't there been anyone special after she'd broken up with David McKay?

She frowned, realizing that it had been a long time since she'd lamented her single-girl status. It had to be because David was back in her life, however temporary that might be. She'd have to be careful. Make sure he didn't think she'd been moping around all these years, waiting for him to come back.

Maybe while she was out on the trail this week she'd figure it all out. In the meantime, she had work to do.

In the stall nearest her, Sheba, her best sorrel mare, nickered a welcome. And farther along, Joe swung his head over the stall door, eager to see if she'd brought treats.

The smell of leather and hay brought back so many happy memories. Sunday afternoons when the four D'Angelo kids had pretended to be Pony Express riders. A rainy Saturday when Rafe had tried to convince her that one of the ponies could read her mind. And later, once David had come into her life, the two of them riding the trails around the lake. Kissing on top of Wildcat Ridge while their horses sidled restlessly beneath them.

No. She really mustn't think of those times right now.

At one end of the barn sat the tack room and feed bins. Brandon, eager to learn more about this part of the business, had already helped her pack the supplies she and Geneva would need, but with David tagging along, she'd better make sure she had extra.

She laid everything out once again, making notes with a pad and pencil she kept in the tack room. She'd have to bring another blanket down from the lodge, even though it was summer. More water. Another set of utensils and dishes. Rations for one more horse and mule.

Would His Royal Hollywood Highness settle for plain old American coffee? He was probably used to some fancy blend. Well, tough. If he didn't like the meals she had planned, he could turn around and go home.

She made a notation on her list, wondering if she could get away with feeding him basic camp food for two weeks. "How do you feel about pork and beans, Mr. Ritz-Carlton?" she said aloud.

To punctuate her displeasure, she drew a

hard line under one of the words she'd written. The point of her pencil broke off with a small snap.

She stared at it, then swore so loudly that Sheba pricked up her ears. Stalking into the tack room, Addy searched in vain for another pencil, a pen, *anything,* but found nothing. More swearing. Why hadn't she cleaned out the drawers so she could find things? Why didn't she plan better?

Disgusted and breathing hard, she sat down on a bale of hay and lowered her head into her hands. She had been afraid of letting go, but now all the unshed tears waiting for a break in her control found their release.

It was ridiculous, but she couldn't seem to stop crying. Ever since she'd walked into Geneva McKay's house and seen David standing there, her emotions had been teetering on the edge of something too heart-wrenching to be ignored.

She felt threatened, endangered, and only pride and her own mulish nature kept her from calling off this whole trip. Maybe she'd do it, and to hell with what he thought.

"Addy?" she heard a quiet voice say.

She jerked her head up to see that Dani had entered the barn. She stood looking at Addy uncomfortably, as if she didn't know whether to back away or come forward. It might have been funny if Addy hadn't felt so miserable.

She made a token attempt to regain control, wiping her eyes with the edge of her T-shirt. "Hi," she said around a sniffle. "You lost?"

"No," her sister-in-law said. "I was actually looking for you. I wanted to see if you were all right."

Addy made a face. She was embarrassed but glad that if anyone had to catch her blubbering like a baby, it was Dani. "Do I *look* all right?"

"No. Is there something I can do to help?"

"Not unless you know a magic trick that can make someone disappear."

"Is this about Geneva's grandson? The fact that he's going on this trip with you?"

"It's that obvious?"

Dani sat down next to her on the hay bale, nudging her gently with her shoulder. "Rafe told me he broke your heart years ago."

"Rafe talks too much all of a sudden."

"Do you want to discuss it?"

"Not much to tell."

"I'm a good listener."

"It's not that exciting."

"Try me," Dani said with an encouraging smile.

Addy shrugged. She supposed there was no harm in telling Dani. She was so new to the family that she'd have no preconceived notions. "David McKay moved here to live with his grandparents after his parents were killed in a car accident. I was in the seventh grade when he showed up in my English class. By the eighth grade I was practicing writing *Mrs. Adriana McKay.*"

Dani laughed a little. "Love at first sight, huh?"

Addy nodded. "For me, anyway. Not for David. He was very popular with all the girls. He was a math wiz, but he really wanted to be a documentary filmmaker. He was so passionate about things. It was one of the ways he was different from everyone else. It was what made him special in my eyes."

"After you left, Geneva was telling us

about the movie that was filmed here and how quickly David made a name for himself once he moved to Hollywood."

"That was really the end for us, that film," Addy said with a sigh. "After he got involved with it he was...different."

"How?" Dani touched her arm sympathetically. "Geneva said David became very good friends with the producer and the crew. That he followed them to Hollywood because he felt he could get an introduction into the business."

"He did. Everything he'd been dreaming of came to him because of that one silly movie."

"An offer he couldn't turn down."

"Of course," Addy admitted. "That's really at the heart of it, you know? That he could run off to Hollywood with those people. We'd been dating steadily. It had never occurred to me that he would ever seriously want to leave here. To leave *me*. But he said it was an opportunity he couldn't pass up. That he'd come back. I was devastated."

"So you fought?"

Addy nodded. "Out by the lake on the night before he left. The things we said to one another were hateful. He accused me of being jealous, not trusting him. Of trying to keep him from achieving his dream. I told him that he'd obviously found a way to use people to get to the top. That he didn't need me any longer since there wasn't a damned thing I could do to help him."

Dani's eyes widened. "Wow. Not a great way to end a relationship."

"No. That was the last time we spoke." Addy raked her fingers through her hair wearily. "And now he's back."

Dani reached out to squeeze her hand. "Do you still love him?" she asked quietly.

Addy's heart bumped a little. Stupid, really, because she knew now that their love had been a fierce, ragged flame destined to go out. "No. But that doesn't mean he can't *get* to me. He's the one I thought I'd spend the rest of my life with. I used to picture the two of us living here, near our families. When he left, I…"

"You what?" Dani asked with a quizzical glance.

"I think I gave up on all of that."

Dani stood, crouching in front of Addy so

that she could take her arms in both hands. She frowned down at her. "It doesn't mean you can't have it with someone else, Addy. You have so much to give a man. One day—"

"One day, one day," Addy mimicked, feeling miserable and mired in the loneliness that now characterized her life. "I don't want to wait any longer to get what you and Rafe have. What Matt's found with Leslie. And Nick with Kari. If I can't have that…"

Neither of them said anything for a few moments. Then Dani spoke. "So you think having a baby of your own, raising a child alone, will make up for not having a man in your life?"

"I think I want *something*. I need to have…" She trailed off with a sigh. "Right now I have to get through *two weeks* with David McKay. And I just don't know how to do that."

Dani gave her a little shake, making Addy look up. "Adriana D'Angelo! Stop talking like such a weakling. You come from one of the toughest, most sensible families I've ever met. You're a helicopter pilot. You run this stable. You're considering being a single parent. You take on responsibilities that would send a weaker woman screaming for help."

"I can make rose radishes and you can't." She gave a watery smile. "That doesn't make me exceptional."

"Well, you are," Dani said. "All right. So this idiot is suddenly in your face again. It shouldn't even be a blip on your radar. You can handle him. So maybe he had the power to turn your knees to jelly ten years ago, but if he thinks you're going to fall for moonlight and roses still, he's dead wrong. You're wiser and he has no power over you. He's just another guest."

"He's more than that."

"No, he's not. Your father would say he's not a problem, he's just a challenge you haven't found an answer for yet."

Losing the impulse to lie, Addy shook her head. "My father doesn't know David McKay was my first lover. The man who got me pregnant."

Dani's mouth parted in surprise. "What?"

"No one knows it, but I miscarried a little boy three days after David left town."

CHAPTER THREE

LATE THAT EVENING, IN her guest bedroom at
Lightning River Lodge, Geneva sat on the
side of the bed and looked down at the box
containing her late husband's ashes. She
didn't really believe Herbert was there. In
fact, she was quite sure he watched over her
from heaven. But when she spoke to him—
and she often did—she liked to have this
touchstone close. She supposed she was
getting old, acting so foolishly sentimental.

"Now don't fret, Herbert," she said. "What
I told David was only a tiny, harmless bit of
deception. He needs this so much. Ulcers
and headaches and wrinkles on his forehead
at his young age—why, our boy's a walking
medical journal."

She wiped a minuscule bit of lint out of a
crevice on the lid. In the early years of their

marriage, back before arthritis had played such havoc with his fingers, Herbert had carved this notions box for her. No one knew that—not even David.

"I miss you so much," she said softly, then shook her head, refocusing her thoughts. "He's not happy, Herbert. All that success, and he's miserable, I tell you. I know you never liked me to meddle, but I just couldn't let it go on without trying to do *something*. I have a good feeling about this trip."

There was a light tap on her bedroom door. She'd been expecting it and she went quickly to answer, pulling the sash of her robe tighter.

"Come in," she said softly. She glanced up and down the hallway. "Did anyone see you?"

"Not a soul," Sam D'Angelo answered with a conspiratorial grin.

SAM HAD SETTLED INTO one of two chairs by the window. He smiled again at Geneva, feeling like a guilty child. He had always been the kind of man who loved intrigue, and lately there had been so little of it in his life. He felt revitalized and excited by the plot he and Geneva had hatched.

"Everyone's asleep," he told Geneva as she took the other chair.

"What about Rose?"

He waved away that concern. "Rosa knows I like to make one last check of the downstairs before I go to bed. She won't suspect a thing."

That was crucial, because if there was one person who could put the brakes on this whole scheme, it was his wife. Sam loved Rosa dearly, but the woman had no sense of adventure and thought people ought to mind their own business. A first-class spoilsport.

A few months ago, Sam had gone to Geneva in secret with the idea of hiring her to paint his wife's portrait. In her younger years, his friend had been Geneva St. John, a fairly well-known artist, and it seemed the perfect gift for Rosa's upcoming birthday.

But as they'd talked, the conversation had stretched into memories of the past, when her grand-son, David, and his only daughter, Adriana, had been so close. They knew that a major argument had taken place, harsh words had been exchanged. But wasn't it a shame that the two families hadn't been connected through marriage after all?

Before the afternoon had gone, they'd agreed that maybe something could be done to change that. Surely enough time had passed. Both their children were unattached. Perhaps because they still cared for one another. Wouldn't it be lovely if that spark between them could be fanned to life again?

Nothing came of that idea until Addy had dropped her bomb about checking out a sperm bank in Denver. It was then that Sam knew it was time to fly into action.

In the end, it had been much easier than they'd expected. A legitimate excuse to hire Addy. A well-timed telephone call to David. The right incentive.

And…here they were.

"How did it go at your place?" Sam asked.

"Tense," Geneva admitted. "I felt like a referee. David was frustrated with both of us. Addy was trying to pretend she wasn't shocked. And did you see how uncomfortable she was tonight whenever David's name came up? You can't tell me they don't feel something for each other anymore."

"I just hope what they feel is enough," Sam said with a shake of his head. He was Italian. He believed in the power of true love. But his daughter could be a stubborn woman sometimes. If her mind was made up about artificial insemination, this could all be wasted effort.

No. He refused to believe that.

Geneva sighed, and Sam knew she agreed. "I do wish David had gotten off to a better start with her. I don't want them to get on each other's nerves so much that they can't see they're still in love. I'll just have to ask Herbert to put a bug in his ear to behave."

Sam rubbed his hands together. "*Dio!* I wish I could make this trip with you."

"Me, too. Can it be a conspiracy if only one person's there to do all the plotting?"

"I'm counting on you," Sam said with a wink. "Addy said she has stops planned along the way to replenish supplies. Think you can slip away once in a while to give me an update on how it's going?"

"I'll certainly try. I just hope we're doing the right thing."

Sam pounded his fist on his thigh. "Damn it! I refuse to see my daughter continue to sit on the shelf like some Victorian spinster or run off to make a baby with a petri dish. D'Angelos are not created in chemistry labs."

"But what if her mind's made up?"

"Impossible! She's confused, conflicted about what she's doing with her life. But once she remembers what it's like with that grandson of yours…" He stood, slipping into his metal crutches. "Well, good luck, G. Don't do anything I wouldn't do."

"I suspect you'd do almost anything."

"True," Sam admitted. "Now I'd better get back to Rosa before she comes looking for me."

"It wouldn't do for her to find you in my room," Geneva said with a light laugh.

"Ha!" Sam said. "Rosa knows the only woman who's a threat to her is Sophia Loren." He leaned over to hug Geneva. "Be careful out there."

Sam made his way back to his own bedroom. The lights were off, but he didn't need them. After all these years of sleeping beside the same woman, he knew where everything was, what obstacles to watch out for.

As he slipped quietly into bed, Rosa turned toward him. "What took you so long?" she asked in a sleepy tone.

"Just making my last check of the evening."

"I thought you did that while I took my shower," she said, a frown in her voice. She rubbed her hand along his chest. "It was nice spending time with Geneva tonight, wasn't it? We should invite her to come up more often."

"Definitely."

"I do think the two of you were a little insensitive to Addy's feelings about David. I suppose you just got carried away, but it was hard for her to hear so much about him and how he's been doing."

"Well, maybe there's a good reason for that," Sam said. "Maybe she ought to think about giving David another chance."

Rosa came up on one elbow, and if there had been enough light in the room, Sam guessed he'd have seen a frown creasing her brow. "Do you know something I don't?"

"Of course not. Go back to sleep, Rosie." He turned back to snuggle against the only woman he had ever loved. The kind of love his daughter should have in her life. If it was a baby she wanted, why couldn't it be made with a loving husband?

"I'm glad to see you've stopped badgering her about her decision to have a baby alone if she chooses. Have you accepted that it's really none of our business?"

"No. When your child is about to take a leap off a steep cliff, as a parent, don't you have a responsibility to at least *try* to grab their coattail?" Then, thinking that he'd revealed too much, he flipped on his side in an effort to halt the conversation. His wife could read him like a book sometimes. "Never mind that now," Sam said. "I'm tired. Good night, Rosa."

AT DAYBREAK THE NEXT morning a cab delivered David and his things to Lightning River Lodge's front door.

The place looked just the way he remembered it. Maybe a little timeworn, but that only enhanced its rustic elegance and the way it seemed to fit in with its surroundings.

He considered going inside, since he wouldn't have minded paying a visit to the D'Angelos. He thought of Sam and Rose as nice people with big hearts. They reminded David of his own parents.

A quick glance at his watch told him there was no time for that now. He was close to being late. That wouldn't do for trail-boss Addy, he'd bet.

The pile of supplies at his feet had been pulled together by a miraculous feat of determination on his part. For the first time in years he'd had to hustle to make things happen, because he didn't have his flock of well-paid flunkies traipsing after him. But he'd decided to treat it as a challenge. One of many he'd probably have to face before this trip was over.

All in all, he felt pretty pleased with himself.

Of course, given the size and selection of Broken Yoke's shopping district, he hadn't been able to be too particular in his choice of suitable clothing. He knew he resembled a tinhorn tourist: new designer jeans, expensive boots and a Stetson that hadn't had the chance to shape a personality of its own yet.

As for the demands of business...well, he was still working out the kinks on that front. He hadn't taken a real vacation in years, and when he'd told his assistant Rob just what he had planned for the next two weeks, the man had been practically speechless. It might be days before all the bases were covered back in his Los Angeles office, but he'd manage. He always did.

Quickly David strapped everything to his body so he could make the walk down to the stable. He felt like a damned pack mule and he knew he looked ridiculous.

As he approached the corral, Addy D'Angelo glanced up from her clipboard. Seeing him, she scowled. It didn't take much imagination to guess her thoughts. She'd been hoping he wouldn't show up.

Too bad, trail boss. You're stuck with me.

She was dressed much as she had been yesterday, practical and trim in jeans and a thin blouse. Today her hair was captured in a ponytail, yanked low at the back of her head. Disappointing. It was one of her best assets, that hair. If he really had to go on this foolhardy outing, it wouldn't have hurt to have something nice to look at.

"You're late," she remarked, then turned her attention back to her list.

"Hey, cut me some slack," David complained as he plopped his duffel bag on the ground. "I was up until two this morning getting everything ready."

His grandmother came out of the stable with a nice-looking guy dressed like the Marlboro Man. David bent to brush a kiss against her cheek. "Morning, Gran. Haven't changed your mind by any chance, have you?"

"Oh, heavens no," she exclaimed. "I'm itchin' to make tracks. That's cowboy lingo," she confided in a mischievous tone. "Brandon taught me." She touched the sleeve of the man by her side. "This is Brandon O'Dell, David. He runs the front desk, but lately he's been helping out here at the stable. Brandon, my overprotective grandson David."

The two men shook hands. The guy fit the cowboy profile. Strong, silent type. He excused himself quickly to check one of the horse's saddles.

Gran straightened as if for inspection. "How do I look?"

David slid his sunglasses down his nose. She wore pink polyester slacks, a gaily colored blouse with lace at the collar and cuffs and an enormous sun hat held on by a lavender ribbon tied under her chin. *Like an explosion in a flower garden,* he thought. *God help us.*

He smiled his approval. "Just like Annie Oakley."

Looking pleased, Gran went to a spotted horse that was tied to the corral railing and fed the animal a few carrots. Beside it, a fine-boned mare with a blaze down its face stamped impatiently. A little way off, Addy began to work on the pack of a mule that looked as if it could think of better things to do so early in the morning.

"Cut it out, Bounder," Addy commanded, kneeing the mule in the belly so that the animal grunted and sucked air. David watched Addy retighten the cinch with quick, efficient movements.

"Need any help?" he asked, feeling that he should at least make the offer even though he knew she didn't need it with O'Dell there. Coming from him, she probably wouldn't have accepted it anyway.

"Nope." She squinted down at the little

mountain of luggage he'd brought. "Too much stuff."

"Only the necessities.'

"Did you keep to my list?"

"Pretty much."

She jerked her head toward the black canvas tote that sat on top of his duffel bag. "What's in there?"

"My laptop."

She turned an astounded look his way. "A computer." She shook her head. "No way."

He'd expected her objection and prepared for it. "I have obligations. I can work in the evening after we've camped and communicate with my office by cellular modem. None of it will interfere with your plans on this trip."

She gave the mule's cinch a final yank, then turned toward David. Those lovely dark eyes sparked with hot, piercing lights. "My mule isn't a four-legged secretary who's going to fetch and carry your office equipment."

"Fine. Loan me a backpack and I'll carry it myself."

"It stays here."

"It goes," he countered in the same dead-level tone.

"David, I'm not just being stubborn about this. We pack light by necessity."

"You've allowed Gran to bring her flower press and sketch book."

Color flew up her cheeks, and he felt the solid power of her antagonism. She gave him a serpentine smile. "You want to bring your flower press? Feel free."

He sighed and shook his head, then pulled the brochure she'd given him yesterday out of his jeans pocket. He held it up in front of her and removed his sunglasses. "It says here, 'Guests participating in overnight pack trips may bring items of personal entertainment such as paperback books, personal stereos and games as long as said items do not disrupt the enjoyment of other campers *or exceed five pounds per person.*"

"Yes, but—"

David rammed the brochure back into his pocket and with the tip of his fingers lifted the computer satchel. "Even with the extra batteries I brought, this weighs only three and a half. I checked."

He heard O'Dell chuckle behind him. "He's got you there, Ad," the man said as he came around them to tie off one of the mule lines.

Addy made a face at the man. "Whose side are you on?"

"The customer is always right."

I like this guy, David thought. *Why can't he be the one to take Gran out on this trip?*

With a frown, Addy yanked on one of the reins tied to the hitching post. "Let's go. We're burning daylight."

They mounted and settled into their saddles with the usual last-minute adjustments for stirrups and reins. And then a strange thing happened. Brandon O'Dell put his hand on Addy's jeans-clad leg to catch her attention.

"Take it easy out there," he told her.

She nodded, and he pulled her down to his level for a quick kiss.

Whoa, cowboy. It was almost over before it happened, but David caught it. It confused the heck out of him.

They all turned into the trail that led away from the corral. Day one of a two-week journey into folly. And all David could think was, *What kind of ranch hand gets to kiss the trail boss goodbye?*

ADDY SET THE PACE ON Sheba and tugged a lazy Bounder behind her by a guide rope tied to her saddle. Geneva, appearing to be a surprisingly capable rider, had fallen in after her on Clover, and David brought up the rear on Injun Joe, leading Little Legs, the second pack mule.

The laptop computer had been slipped into a spare backpack, and, giving her a look that indicated its weight was insignificant, David had fit it onto his shoulders.

We'll see, she thought. *After a few days on the trail, that pack will feel like it's filled with bricks.*

She wondered what kind of trip this would turn out to be. She should have insisted Brandon come along. But he'd said the lodge was too busy right now to be short even one person.

Since they'd added overnight camping trips to the lodge's amenities, she'd dealt with all kinds of guests—weekend warriors eager to play cowboy, know-it-alls who bored everyone, male chauvinists who didn't want to take direction from a woman and even an occasional letch who pinched her rear end as she saddled the horses.

But not one of them had ever been an ex-lover. How did you make innocent small talk around the campfire when you shared *that* kind of history?

Last night Dani had convinced Addy that she could handle whatever happened in the next two weeks. She was tough. Resilient. She didn't have to worry about being around David McKay. She could take whatever he wanted to dish out.

Swearing Dani to secrecy about the miscarriage, Addy had pulled herself together. This morning she just hoped that her determination could stick.

Under the pretense of checking Bounder's lead, Addy swung around in the saddle. Geneva sat, brightly observant of everything around her. Behind the old woman, David had coaxed Joe into an easy walk.

She had to admit he still had his riding seat. He didn't slump or hold the reins high and loose. His extremely broad, masculine chest, with its glimpse of dark hair above the sharply pressed blue shirtfront, remained perfectly still as his hips swayed slightly to match Joe's gait.

He looked bored. It was hard to tell because the sunglasses were back in place. When he realized that Addy was watching him, he lifted his hand in a wave and smiled a smile too wide for sincerity.

In that moment there was a little trill of sound, like a songbird's call. In astonishment Addy watched as David pulled a cellular phone out of his shirt pocket and proceeded to carry on a conversation with someone named Rob.

She was speechless.

Geneva had turned in her saddle, as well. Spying the telephone, she said, "Oh, David. I should have known…."

Refusing to allow her own exasperation to show, Addy faced the trail again.

What had she been worried about? This wasn't a guy she couldn't resist. *This* David McKay was someone she didn't know—an obnoxious, arrogant toad.

The next two weeks were going to be a snap.

CHAPTER FOUR

LIGHTNING RIVER LODGE sat above the town of Broken Yoke, on the edge of the front range. Since its nearest neighbor was at least a mile away, it took surprisingly little time to leave the rest of civilization behind.

By way of well-worn wagon trails and hiking paths, they traveled along the rim of the Arapahoe National Forest and passed only four other people on horseback.

Addy had promised Geneva that she would map out a route to the Devil's Smile that would replicate the McKays' original honeymoon trip as closely as possible. With the exception of two spots along the way where progress had encroached on the backcountry and the necessary stops to replenish supplies, it was conceivable they could make the entire journey without seeing any other human beings.

Around noon Addy pulled Sheba and Bounder out of the lineup, indicating to Geneva that she should continue in the lead.

"How are you holding up?" she asked as the other woman rode past.

"Just fine, dear," Geneva replied.

"How about some lunch? There's a pretty clearing up ahead where we can stop."

The sun hat bobbed up and down as Geneva nodded agreement.

As David's horse came abreast of Addy's, she swung in beside him. After having to listen to him talk on his cell phone all morning, she was glad to see that, for the moment, he'd put away the earpiece that had seemed welded to his ear. However, she noticed that he was now busy with his PDA, his stylus moving so quickly across the pad that he might have been playing video games.

It was maddening to watch.

"Ready to take a break?" she asked, trying not to let her irritation show. The two weeks ahead of them would go a lot faster if they weren't constantly at odds with one another.

"You're the boss," he replied with a shrug.

"There's a good spot up ahead to have lunch." The phone in his shirt pocket rang again, and Addy arched an eyebrow his way. "Or maybe you'd like to call for a pizza delivery."

He wedged the earpiece back into his ear, listened for a moment or two, then said, "Rob, let me call you back. I'm in the middle of something right now."

"Don't stop on my account," Addy said with an air of indifference as he clicked off the phone and removed his sunglasses.

He watched her with a keen, dark interrogation. "You're annoyed with me," he stated.

She hesitated only a moment before she shrugged and said, "Not annoyed. Just a little disappointed."

"Disappointed?"

"Don't you remember what this area is like? On this trip we're going to pass through some of the most beautiful untamed country in Colorado. But you're not going to see any of it because you'll be too busy with conference calls or crunching numbers on your computer or sending faxes—"

"I didn't bring my portable fax attachment," he cut in. His expressive mouth had gathered into amused lines.

"What a concession!"

"I think so."

She gave him a tight, disgusted look. "The rich, powerful businessman. How does it feel to be a living cliché?"

Immediately Addy knew that remark had hit its target. A person who hadn't known David so well might not have guessed. But she saw it—the slight narrowing of his eyes, the way his shoulders straightened.

"Look," he said with exaggerated patience, "I like Colorado. I know it's beautiful, so you don't have to sell me on that. And, truthfully, I can use a vacation. But you don't have to make it your personal responsibility that I enjoy this."

"As if I would."

One dark eyebrow lifted in lazy good humor. "You think you've won, don't you? But I'm hoping that in a day, maybe two, Gran will realize there are easier, faster ways to accomplish what she wants, and we'll be heading back the way we came."

She felt a quiet, scorching anger toward

him in that moment and she didn't try to hide it. "Right now your grandmother sees this trip as the most important thing in her life. Just for a little while, why don't you try to pretend this isn't all about you?"

He said nothing. His gaze moved over her face, and she felt oddly unsettled under his scrutiny.

With his grandmother still out of earshot, he said, "I don't really want to fight with you, Addy, and I'm sure you mean well. I'm just not willing to take chances with Gran's health."

"Neither am I," Addy tossed back. "I think I know her physical limitations. Probably better than you do. Where were you when she had heart surgery last year?" She snapped her fingers. "Oh, that's right. Out of the country on business."

She heard his breathing change and knew she'd gone too far. But really, what right did he have to act as though she didn't give a damn about Geneva's health?

The silence went to foolish lengths, and Addy began to feel a touch of embarrassment and guilt. Hadn't Geneva once told her that she'd deliberately instructed her doctors *not* to notify David about her heart surgery?

Oh Lord, she couldn't remember. But if he hadn't known, why didn't he say something to defend himself now? Why didn't he tell her she was out of line? At the very least, why didn't he stop looking at her like that, as though she was someone he'd never seen before?

Annoyed with herself as much as him, Addy squared her shoulders and looked him straight in the eye. If she let him get to her after less than a day on the trail, two weeks was going to seem like a lifetime.

Where are you, Dani, when I need your lecture about being able to handle this man?

"Listen," she said and then took a deep breath. "Clover's gait is the smoothest in our stable, and she's got a soft mouth, so your grandmother won't have to do more than crook a finger to get her to respond. I've built in downtime in camp so that she doesn't exhaust herself. You and I could probably make it to the canyon in less than a week, but we'll take this much slower. I've packed extra cushioning for her bedroll and I have a few other surprises for her that ought to make things easier."

"Sounds like you've thought of everything," he said, and this time she heard no telltale trace of mockery in his tone.

"I've tried to. In spite of the way everything turned out for…for us, I've always remained very fond of your grandmother."

She started to pull away, but he reached across the distance that separated them, halting her with one hand over hers on Sheba's reins. "Addy…"

She waited, braced for some cutting remark. And yet, for a moment it was the touch of his hand on hers that she was most aware of. She felt suddenly filled with a sharp, nameless anxiety.

"I appreciate your efforts," he said at last.

She moistened her lips, wondering if her cheeks were as pink as they felt. "I'll do my part," she promised, her voice taking on a brisk note to keep from revealing her surprise. "You try to do yours."

"What's my part?" he asked, releasing his hold to sit back in the saddle.

"For your grandmother's sake, pretend to have a good time."

He laughed. "It would be a lot easier if you

hadn't given me a mount who tries to drop his nose every five minutes to crop grass."

"Don't let him. You're the one in charge."

He cocked his head to one side and favored her with a look that made a finger of curling heat spread through her insides. "Really?" he remarked. "I thought *you* were, trail boss."

She pressed her lips together and glanced down, finding sudden interest in threading Sheba's reins through her fingers. Fortunately Geneva saved her from having to come up with an appropriately clever response. Twisting around to glance their way, she asked, "What are you two up to back there?"

The moment passed. In a strong, steady voice, Addy replied, "David was just telling me he's getting saddle sore. We'd better take a break and let him stretch out the kinks."

THE TRUTH WAS, BY THE end of the day when they stopped to set up camp by a winding stream, David wasn't saddle sore. He was *in agony*.

His neck and shoulders were on fire. A

hitching pain knifed into his side, and his butt felt as though a boxer had used it for a punching bag. He might not have forgotten how to ride, but he'd definitely forgotten how much a couple thousand pounds of horse-flesh between your legs could realign your skeletal system.

Not surprisingly, Addy didn't seem to be suffering any discomfort. David was irritated to witness the agility with which she slid off her horse and began tethering the animals. Gran didn't seem much affected, either. She slipped off Clover before anyone could furnish a hand to help her down.

David dismounted with an inward sigh of relief and a stretch of weariness. He was tired. Tired of trail dust and the monotonous thud of horse's hooves. Tired of fielding questions and solving problems for his office that should have been handled in person.

Most of all, he was tired of watching Addy's shapely little behind rock gently back and forth in her saddle.

He had tried to tell himself that he was probably just bored. There was no reason for that slight, sensual movement of hers to take him by the throat this way. None at all.

And definitely no reason for him to still be remotely curious about the relationship between Addy and Brandon O'Dell. Close friends? New lovers? What?

Gran had been no help in shedding any light. One of the few times he'd managed to get her out of Addy's earshot to ask, she'd responded with a shrug and said he'd have to ask Addy himself. Gran could be the sphinx when she wanted to be.

Removing his Stetson, David ran one hand across the back of his neck. Sunburned, probably.

"I'll take care of the horses if you'll put up the tent," Addy told him. He nodded agreement, and she tossed back the waterproof cover over Sheba's pack to withdraw a small hammer and the nylon bag holding the tent, stakes and struts.

"What can I do to help?" Geneva piped in. "And don't tell me to rest."

"We'll need a fire," Addy said. "Scout around for deadwood and a few small twigs to use for kindling. I brought some homemade chicken and dumplings that will need to be heated. And we'll need hot water to wash up later."

Geneva set off on her assignment while Addy began unsaddling the horses and mules. David glanced around the spot she'd chosen as their campsite.

She knew what she was doing. It was pretty and practical, a sheltered circle of large boulders and pines with a level grassy area ideal for the tent. The nearby stream was meandering, the current so sluggish and smooth that the reflection of the cottonwood trees along the bank seemed enameled on its surface.

It was early yet. The sun still held a bright, burnished shimmer overhead and wouldn't set for at least an hour.

He shook out the tent, which seemed to be one of those fancy dome-type ones that took a minimum of work to erect once you got the hang of it.

The first time he smacked one of the stakes with the hammer, it bounced straight back at him and almost took out an eye. Determined, he attacked the hard ground with the hammer's head until he'd dug a hole. Maybe there was a better way, but he wasn't about to ask for directions.

Thirty minutes later the little clearing had been turned into a neat and orderly campsite. The horses and mules were hobbled and munching contentedly on grain. His grandmother was stirring a pot of dumplings over the fire. Indian blankets had been spread. Addy was in the tent, laying out pads and bedrolls and affixing a battery-powered lantern to one of the tent struts.

Glancing around at what the three of them had achieved, David wondered if maybe this trip wouldn't be such a disaster after all.

The evening scents began to awaken and wander through the air. The wind died, making the extra clothing they'd pulled out of their packs unnecessary. They ate the dumplings with coffee and warmed corn bread brought from the lodge and talked of inconsequential things—the few glimpses of wildlife they'd seen today, the chance for rain. The likelihood of getting a good night's sleep in strange surroundings and unfamiliar bedding.

Every so often Gran seemed inclined to turn the conversation to the past, but David noticed that Addy was quick to change the subject. If she hadn't, he knew he would have. No point in reliving any of that, now, was there?

After dinner Gran disappeared into the tent. Addy set another pot over the fire to heat water for dish washing and bathing. When that was done, she joined his grandmother and then emerged moments later with a small toiletry bag.

"I'll be sleeping out here tonight," she told him.

"Why? We can squeeze three people in the tent."

"On trips like this I usually sleep under the stars. I like the feel of the night breeze on my face."

"Suppose it rains?"

"Then I'll come inside." When she saw his eye-brows knit in a solid line, she added, "Look, you don't have to worry about your macho image on this trip. I don't expect you to be uncomfortable for my sake."

"I've slept out in the open plenty of times," he protested tersely.

"Recently?"

"No."

"Well, I do it all the time now, so I'm used to it. And I happen to like it."

He shrugged. "Fine. Let's take turns, then."

With a resigned sigh, she said, "All right. Every other night I'll sleep in the tent with your grandmother."

"Starting tonight," he added.

With an agreement reached, she moved toward the fire.

David watched her tend the campfire and send a plume of sparks skyward to meet the heavens. She'd lost the ponytail, and the rippling fall of her hair was full of fiery highlights. The glow of the flames reflected off her features, making her cheeks gleam like satin and painting the curve of her throat with golden light.

He stared down into his coffee cup, his heart jerking.

David appreciated the sight of a beautiful woman. And no doubt about it, Addy still had prettiness to spare. In fact, it didn't seem as though she'd changed one bit in the time he'd been gone.

He hadn't seriously dated in months,

content to take refuge in the satisfaction of hard work and the respect he received for his accomplishments. That was all he needed. That was what he knew.

All right, so maybe lately it felt as though his life had lapsed into a narrow rut, full of pools he never had time to swim in and new cars that sat in garages like zoo animals. Although dissatisfaction was inevitable once in a while, he had found that discontent eventually became a comfortable, familiar routine.

And when he felt the need to be lifted out of his circumstances, there were always females circling him like honeybees. That was one thing about the women in Hollywood. They had plenty of aggressive ambition.

But certainly he was well over any interest in Addy D'Angelo.

So stop looking for trouble, pal. Think about something else.

With an abrupt movement, he rose, as if that was all it would take to cease to know Addy's existence.

She rocked back on her heels and looked up at him questioningly.

"Fire's too hot to sit so close," he said, hoping that he'd managed to keep his expression flat and uninterpretable. "And I have work to do."

He retrieved his laptop and one of the lanterns. A few feet away from the campfire he found a perfect spot where he could keep an eye on things but might be spared the constant reminder of Addy's disturbing presence.

The Peterson agreement. Ten minutes of the new catering contract for his production company would be enough to capture his interest and kill what was left of the evening.

His grandmother was already snoring softly when Addy rummaged through the supply box for something, then disappeared into the tent. Shadows danced in the lantern light as she moved around inside.

Good. Day one almost over, David thought as he pulled up the Peterson file on his computer. He didn't need to spend any more time being sociable or helpful tonight.

Thirteen days to go. Way to go, McKay.

The night air seemed full of sweetness, and down by the stream a frog chorus had begun a serenade. Moonbeams braided through the clouds overhead. Perfect.

David situated himself into a comfortable position and began tapping out changes to the terms of the deal his legal team had prepared. He intended to offer it to Peterson by phone tomorrow morning.

Witness that the said first party, McKay Worldwide Inc., does hereby acknowledge unto the said second party—

He heard a muffled groan of pleasure and looked up. He could tell from the shadows on the tent wall that it was Addy, massaging lotion into her shoulders and arms.

Whereas the party of the second part, Peterson Catering, has agreed to accept a payment in the amount of—

At the sound of a tiny sigh of relaxation, he glanced up again. She was still at it.

—one hundred and eighty-seven thousand dollars, to be paid over a period not to exceed three months, the first monthly installment being due and payable on the twenty-first of August—

In his peripheral vision David caught a flicker of light. He tilted his head toward the tent. Elongated shadows on the tent surface indicated that Addy had risen. He could see the outlined thrust of her breasts as she stretched and lifted the heavy sweep of hair off her neck.

Willing away that awareness, David lowered his eyes to the computer. The cursor blinked at him as if irritated. He backspaced and tried to pull concentration around him like a cloak. He red-lined the amount Legal had negotiated and began typing in the amount he intended to offer.

One hundred and fifty-five thousand dollars—

He sat there, suspended, listening to the sudden mad knocking in his chest as he tried to remember what he'd intended to type next.

One hundred and fifty-five thousand—

One hundred and—

With a small noise of self-disgust and a flick of his wrist, he closed the file and shut down the computer. How was a person supposed to concentrate here?

Shoving the laptop back into its case, he rose. He hadn't even gotten control of his frenzied breathing enough to think, but one thing David knew for sure—he needed to get away from the suffocating enclosure of the campsite for a while.

"I'm going for a walk," he called, setting out immediately.

Every muscle seemed to ache with bow-strung tension as, impelled by the blind instinct of flight, he followed the course of the stream. It was fortunate the moon was so bright. The last thing he needed right now was to get lost and have to count on Addy to rescue him.

He stopped to sit on a huge boulder, listening to the sounds of night creatures looking for a new darkness to call home.

And trying to cool the fire in his blood.

He didn't need this kind of excitement. He had enough things to think about on this trip without indulging fantasies about Addy's bare body silhouetted in lamplight. What he could use right now was a session with a very good bottle of booze or a punishing workout at the gym. Maybe a cold shower that would leave a numbness for which he would be eternally grateful...

With an abrupt explosion of movement,

David toed off his boots and socks, ripped his jeans down his legs and pulled off his shirt. Before he could change his mind, he waded naked into the stream.

It took his breath away.

It laid gooseflesh along his spine.

It chattered his teeth.

It was...perfect.

CHAPTER FIVE

DAVID HAD EXPECTED TO spend the night tossing and turning or at the very least to wake up twisted like a pretzel. Instead, after that dip in the icy river, he'd slept well and awoken feeling refreshed, recalled to earth by the sound of Addy banging on an iron pot and calling encouragingly, "Rise and shine, you two. Breakfast in fifteen minutes!"

Gran emerged from the tent, seemingly no worse for wear. She greeted David and Addy with a cheerful, "Good morning!" and then hurried to the makeshift lavatory they'd created last night: a plastic basin for a sink and a small mirror wedged into a tree. A bent branch became a towel rack.

David rolled over within his sleeping bag, surprised to discover that while he'd been sound asleep out in the open, only a few feet away Addy had started a fire, coffee and the beginnings of breakfast. She was also dressed in fresh jeans and a T-shirt, and her hair, shining in the morning sun, lay smoothly brushed against her back. Compared to her bright efficiency, he felt every bit the disheveled tenderfoot slug.

Since he had slept in his underwear, he slipped into the tent while Addy was busy pouring coffee into mugs. His duffel bag had been wedged into a corner, and he dug it out, searching for clean clothes.

The tent flap lifted and suddenly Addy was there. "How about a cup of coffee?" Her quick glance took in his state of undress. "Oops, sorry. I thought you'd slept in your clothes."

He refused to act like a timid virgin in her presence. After all, once upon a time they'd seen each other in even less. Nonchalantly he reached out to take the mug from her hands. "You know, just because we're out in the wilderness, that doesn't mean we have to abandon good manners. Like knocking before you enter a man's bedroom."

"Well, technically it's still *my* bedroom.

Until tonight, when it's your turn to sleep inside."

She looked him up and down, and in the shadowed interior of the tent he couldn't tell if he'd been found lacking or not. He knew he didn't have the body of an eighteen-year-old anymore, but it couldn't be that bad. He'd have been looking for a new personal trainer if it had been.

"Still wearing boxers, huh?" she said with an arch look. "I thought for sure you'd have switched to briefs."

Beginning to feel at a disadvantage, he straightened as much as the tent would allow. "There's nothing 'brief' about me, and you damned well know it."

She looked uncertain for a moment. Then she gave a healthy hoot of laughter, shook her head and disappeared from the tent's opening.

By the time he was dressed, Gran was finished with her morning routine, and it was his turn. With toothbrush, toothpaste and razor in hand, he positioned himself in front of the plastic basin.

As he shaved, he became aware that he'd angled the mirror so that he had an uninterrupted view of Addy sitting cross-legged before the fire. His brow furrowed in sudden irritation with himself.

But he didn't realign the mirror.

Why couldn't she have turned into some sort of frazzled, leathery earth mother after all this time?

It would have made everything so much easier.

IN TWO DAYS' TIME David realized that they had left National Forest land, with its scenic overlooks and designated hiking trails, and entered the wilder mist-shrouded forests that made up the fringe of the Rockies. Tall ponderosa pines and aspens whispered overhead as their branches were caught by a light breeze that hinted at rain, but for most of the morning the air carried the intoxicating scents of summer.

By lunchtime the sights and sounds of civilization had faded into the distance, and with the exception of David's cellular phone ringing occasionally to remind them of their link to the outside world, they might have been the only three people on the planet.

The trail had widened, so that it was no longer necessary to follow one another nose-to-tail. They rode three abreast, Addy and David positioned on either side of Gran like guardian angels. For David, it was much more preferable than spending the day choking back trail dust.

Unfortunately his conversations with Los Angeles became nearly impossible, since the two women had decided to pass the time by singing every Broadway show tune they could remember—in keys that were not *completely* compatible.

Acknowledging the futility of trying to get any work done until they'd exhausted at least fifty years of musical history, he plopped the cell phone into his shirt pocket. His last battery was giving out anyway, and until they reached the next supply stop, it was probably a good idea to trim his usage.

"Oh, good," Gran said in delight when she realized they had his undivided attention. "David, sing the captain's part while I do Maria. You know how good I used to be with *The Sound of Music.*"

"I've long forgotten the words," he

replied. And then, because he was eager to keep her from pursuing the idea, David said to Addy, "Did I ever tell you that Gran was the darling of the dinner-theater circuit in Arizona? When I was little, I thought sure she'd run off to Broadway and leave Grampa Herb and me behind."

"Oh, as if they would ever have given me a second look," the old woman said, but she pinkened with pleasure at the memory.

"I'll do Captain von Trapp," Addy offered. She clucked encouragement to Bounder, who had fallen behind and was now pulling the lead rope taut.

Gran sang a few words from "Edelweiss," then broke off suddenly. "David, remember when the boy playing Kurt got the flu?" To Addy she said, "We were desperate, and David knew all the parts from listening to me practice. So I dragged him down to the theater, threw him into costume and pushed him onstage at the last minute."

"And it worked?"

Gran and David exchanged knowing glances.

"Couldn't remember a word," Geneva said

with an indulgent shake of her head. "Poor boy stood there like a rabbit caught in car headlights and had to be carried off the stage by all the other children."

Addy burst out laughing. "And I'll bet he looked so cute in his little lederhosen."

"The girl playing Liesl ad-libbed that her little brother suffered from some mysterious paralyzing illness," Gran added.

David couldn't hold back a silly grin. "Little brats. I still can't hear 'Edelweiss' without breaking into a cold sweat."

The three of them laughed together then, and the sound of it, the warm sunshine and the sense of complete isolation made for a powerful combination. Gran began to sing again in a soft, unclouded way, and Addy joined in. With an odd, unexpected feeling of contentment within him, David found his old singing voice—rough and awkward from years of disuse but not unpleasant to the ear all the same.

"SINGING!" SAM GROWLED into the phone. "What good is singing together? We need kisses."

While David and Addy were taking care of their own issues at a rustic camp store they'd stopped at, Geneva had called Sam. He'd slipped into the kitchen pantry for privacy. On the other end, he heard Geneva sigh. "Don't be so impatient. It's too soon for kisses."

"We don't have all year, Geneva."

"I know that. But it needs to be a gradual reawakening between them, Sam. And alone time for the two of them is hard to arrange."

"Well, they're alone now, aren't they?" Realizing that his voice had been too loud and someone might hear, Sam turned toward the pantry wall. "You slipped away. Do more of that."

"I'm doing the best I can. If I'm too obvious, they'll run away from each other like scalded cats."

"Yes," Sam had to agree. "Adriana is a stubborn one. Gets that from her mother."

"David did ask me about Addy's relationship with Brandon. He said he was just curious, but I don't know…."

"That's a good sign."

"I suppose. They're both so impossible.

Addy spends most of her time pretending David doesn't exist, and David is wedded to his cell phone and computer."

"Throw them in the next river you come to. Get rid of them."

"I can't. It's like they're his children."

"Find a way."

"How?"

"You're old and getting feebleminded—"

"I beg your pardon," Geneva said, sounding offended.

"You know…" Sam went on, feeling frustrated that he wasn't out there so that things could be managed to his liking. He'd have had Adriana and David back together before they ever reached the Devil's Smile. "You borrow his phone and then you can't remember where you put it. Or you pick up the computer and *accidentally* drop it into the campfire. Things happen."

"That's true. My mind just isn't what it used to be."

Sam laughed lightly. "There you go. I have faith in you. I know you won't let me down."

"I have to go," Geneva said suddenly. "I'll be in touch."

The line went dead, and Sam snapped the phone shut. Well, nothing concrete so far, but Geneva was as determined as he was to see those two together, so she'd come through. Adriana and David didn't stand a chance. He smiled to himself as he turned to leave the pantry.

Rosa stood in the doorway.

"Who won't let you down?" she asked. "About what?"

She didn't look suspicious, only mildly curious, but Sam knew she could be like a terrier with a bone if she smelled mischief.

"Can't a person have a private conversation in this place without everyone listening in like we've got a party line?"

She tilted her head at him. He should have remembered that being cranky with Rosa seldom did any good. "I think that's why you have an office," she said.

"Well…it's always too hot in there."

"You've never complained before."

"That's because I don't like to make a fuss."

She made an incredulous sound. "Since when?"

"All right. If you must know, that was John

at Mountain Produce. I flubbed this week's order and didn't want you to find out."

Rosa frowned, and Sam realized his mistake immediately. He shouldn't have fibbed about anything that involved her kitchen. His wife knew her domain inside and out. "Mountain Produce just delivered an hour ago. There wasn't anything missing."

"Exactly!" Sam said, knowing he was digging himself in deeper. "Because I called in time to get it corrected. I was just thanking John for being so efficient." When Rosa gave him a skeptical look, Sam slapped his hand against his temple. "I think I'll take a short nap. I have a headache."

That, at least, wasn't a lie. He edged past his wife and headed for their private quarters, aware that she watched him the entire way. He certainly hoped that the plan he and Geneva had cooked up for Adriana's and David's sake worked, because if he had to continue to concoct stories like this, there would be nothing but trouble ahead.

ADDY LED THEM TO A wide meadow surrounded on either side by high cliffs covered in a tapestry of interwoven trees and stone. The ground was starred with wildflowers: lupines, red owl clover, wild geraniums and so many black-eyed Susans that Addy thought it looked like a carpet of pirate's gold had been tossed upon the ground.

Seemingly without the least bit of physical discomfort, Geneva slid off Clover and tossed the reins to David.

"I remember this meadow," she said in an excited tone. "Herbert and I spent the night here. I still have some of the wildflowers we picked pressed in a frame back home. Isn't it amazing? After all these years it's just like we left it."

"We can stop for a while," Addy suggested. "Have lunch."

"Oh, yes, could we? I'd so love to get some new specimens to take back. And I want to get this place on film, too."

The matter was settled without another word. Cinches were loosened so the animals could drink their fill of water. David unstrapped the supply box and ice chest, and Addy spread a blanket in the shade. Geneva retrieved her field guide to flowers, her flower press and camcorder.

Addy had brought as much prepared food as she could safely manage, and in no time she had thick ham sandwiches, potato salad and fresh fruit laid out in front of them like a banquet. She poured lemonade into cups and passed them around.

"It's cool but just barely. We're almost out of ice," she said.

David grimaced as he tasted the tepid mixture. "I miss my ice maker."

"What's her name?" Addy couldn't resist teasing. "We should be able to pick up some ice tomorrow. There's a hiking station on the north rim of this canyon. Everything should keep all right in the chest until then."

After lunch Geneva marched out into the meadow, camcorder in hand. David followed her, and Addy listened as he offered advice about finding the right angle, the right light, keeping her hand steady so she didn't blow the shot. But not once did he suggest he shoot the footage for her.

Addy found that a little disturbing. In the old days, he'd had a camera practically attached to the end of his arm. He had played with film the way other kids played with toys.

Maybe he didn't take enjoyment in it anymore.

Well, it was none of her business if he'd lost that interest.

Content to soak up the mild sunshine, Addy eventually dropped to the ground and wrapped her arms around her knees. The earth was soft and warm beneath her jeans. Wildflowers rose up all around her like a pastel tide.

David came back to join her, moving in that loose-limbed way he had. He lowered himself to the ground, one leg cocked up so that his arm could dangle over his knee.

"Gran seems very happy so far," he remarked. He had picked several fuchsia Bigelovii asters and began absently twisting them together.

"I think so," Addy agreed.

Almost obscured in the sea of flowers, they sat together and watched his grandmother move farther down the meadow with a surprisingly sprightly gait.

Addy lifted her head and breathed deeply, as though she could inhale the light. "Mmm. The sun feels good, doesn't it?" she said.

"If we're not careful, we'll be sunburned by the end of this trip."

She was quiet for a while. Plucking a blade of grass, she chewed on the stem, then withdrew it. "Do you ever have fun anymore, David?" she asked. "I mean, I know you travel to lots of exciting places. But is it all just a backdrop for the next business deal or do you really take time to enjoy yourself?"

"I enjoy my work."

"Do you? When I see pictures of you, you're hardly ever smiling. You used to smile a lot."

He turned to look at her with an arched eyebrow. "Do you watch for pictures of me?"

"No. And don't avoid the question."

He snorted. "No one smiles as much as they did when they were eighteen. Back then we had no idea what an ass-kicking life was going to give us. You have to grow up fast in Hollywood."

"I thought Hollywood was the land of dreamers."

"You can have a dream, but you'd better

be able to back it up with something tangible or you get booted to the curb pretty quickly."

He sounded so cynical, so hard. What had life in Hollywood done to him? For years Addy had resisted asking Geneva any questions about David, but now she wished she'd swallowed her pride enough to find out.

Of course, she didn't need to feel sorry for him. He'd made his choice. What had he called it back then? Ah, yes. His golden opportunity.

It surprised her to feel that old resentment slip over her. Shouldn't she have been long over those feelings by now?

"I can't imagine anyone booting you to the curb," she said.

David frowned a little. "I was always a fast learner. Very resilient. Whatever I have now, I earned."

"I'm sure you did. You never lacked for ambition."

It came out sounding like a criticism, but she hadn't meant it that way. If David took offense, he didn't show it. Instead he sighed and tilted his head skyward. "I made some big mistakes in those early days. There are a lot of things I wish I had handled differently. But I can't go back."

It was very still all around them, with only bugs and birds making blithe music. Their spot in the tall grass seemed like a nest, a hidden place for just the two of them. Addy wondered if David felt the same pull of melting luxury as she. Was it possible to be relaxed and aroused all at the same time?

The feeling evaporated as David's cellular phone out-trilled the birdsong. With a bitten-off curse, he retrieved it from his pocket. His office again.

For a change, Addy was almost relieved. It gave her a chance to reassemble her chaotic thoughts. It also offered her the opportunity to leave him. But, strangely, she remained where she was, shredding the blade of grass between her fingertips and softly humming the tunes from *Oklahoma* she had belted out earlier.

"So he went for it," David was saying. "That's great, Rob. Get Legal to go over it one more time, will you? All the usual stips." He listened to his assistant for a few minutes. "What am I doing?" he repeated, and Addy turned her head to witness his mouth spreading into a lavish grin. "I'm sitting waist-deep in a wildflower meadow with a beautiful woman. So unless you've got something of major importance to add, this conversation is over."

Addy's breath became uneven and quick. She drew air deeply to calm herself. That was just the kind of audacious comment she could expect from David. Anything to throw her completely off stride.

Too bad it was working so well.

He snapped the phone shut and set it on the ground beside him. "Sorry," he said. "Now where were we?"

"Back in the saddle," Addy replied.

But when she made a move to rise, he stopped her with one hand on her arm. "Not yet. Let's give Gran a few more minutes."

She settled back, annoyed with herself, with her apparent susceptibility to him. They should go. They needed to be farther along the trail than this by sunset. But she wanted to stay right here, in this warm, scented scrap of heaven.

He returned his attention to the asters he'd

linked together. To her surprise, they were actually becoming a garland in his hands, and she wondered where he'd learned the trick.

He cocked his head in her direction. "You don't think very much of the life I've made, do you?"

She refused to lie. She cleared her voice self-consciously, and in a neutral tone she countered, "It doesn't matter what I think. You're the one who has to live it."

She felt the inadequacy of that response, and apparently so did he. He gave a little laugh of pure ridicule. "Very diplomatic but not very genuine. I'm disappointed. In the old days, you were never afraid to express your opinion."

"This isn't the old days."

"No, it isn't," he agreed with a sad smile. "But humor me."

"You used to want to make films that meant something," she said quickly before she lost her nerve. "That made a statement. What happened?"

"The films I produce make statements."

"What statement did *The Curse of Ransom Heights* make?" she asked, referring to his production company's movie last year about ghosts in a police station.

He chuckled. "It made the statement that people are suckers for a story that scares the crap out of them. That they'll do anything to feel something, *anything* that will take them out of their mundane little lives for a while."

She stared at him, stunned.

He shot her a frown. "Don't look at me like that. You think I should be doing films about the mating habits of the male ibis? Or who's going to teach Johnny to read if his little one-room schoolhouse gets shut down? No one really cares anymore, Addy. For every cute and cuddly *March of the Penguins* that hits it big, there are ten dockers—documentary filmmakers—out there who have a story no one will ever see. It certainly doesn't get you anywhere."

"And that's the most important thing? Getting somewhere? I would think with the life you've had, there must be damned few destinations left to run to anymore."

He frowned as though he might argue that comment. He had finished connecting both ends of the circlet of flowers and stared down at it in silence for a long time.

He turned toward her at last. "You haven't changed. You were always good at asking the hard questions."

"You used to be a lot better at answering them."

"I'm out of practice," David conceded. "Not many people give me an argument anymore."

"Your grandmother says you work too hard."

"It takes hard work to be successful."

"That's not the same thing. So you'll be the richest, most powerful man in the cemetery. As Geneva's said, you only get so many years here and you ought to spend them doing something you can feel good about. Something that makes you happy."

He shook his head. "That's very simplistic logic."

"Just because it's simple doesn't mean it doesn't work," she said, her voice a gentle reproof. "Maybe you're just too used to seeing ulterior motives and hidden agendas in everything."

"So you think I should just chuck it all?"

he asked, scanning her with sardonic amusement. "Come back here and learn to weave baskets that I can sell on the side of the road?"

"I said simple, not impossible. Remember, I've seen the clay pots you used to throw in art class."

"And I've seen yours," he protested. His face was all laughing for one moment, and then his features went still. After a while, he shifted. "So now I figure it's my turn."

"Your turn for what?"

"To ask questions. Here's one for starters. What's the deal with Brandon O'Dell?"

She hadn't been expecting that. She should probably tell him it wasn't any of his business, but somehow she liked that he was curious.

"Brandon wants to partner with me in running the stable."

"That's all? Looked a little friendlier than that back at the barn."

"Well, he wants to marry me, too."

He looked up at her quickly. "You two are getting married?"

"I don't know. I'm still considering it."

"Wow. Not a lot of passion in that response."

"Passion is for teenagers." And then, because that statement reminded her of how often she and David had been locked in their own passionate embrace years ago, Addy added, "Brandon is a wonderful man. Kind and patient. He'd be a good husband and he'll make a great father."

David studied her for a long moment, as though absorbing her. "Are you saying you're pregnant?"

No reason not to tell him, she guessed. "Not yet. But soon, I hope. Whether I end up marrying Brandon or not, I'm thinking about artificial insemination."

David didn't try to hide his surprise. He flattened his eyebrows and stared at her. "You want a baby that badly?"

She made a face at him. "You say that like I'm going to steal one out of a hospital. It's not that unusual these days for a single woman to go that route, you know. I'm twenty-eight. If I'm going to have children, I need to get started soon." Seeing his reaction, she exhaled a sigh. "Oh, I know it's no use talking to *you* about children. You'd never understand. You hate kids."

He looked even more shocked. "Who said I hated kids?"

"You did. Don't you remember? Back when we were dating you said kids were nothing but hard work and dream-squashers."

"I never said that."

"Believe me, you did."

"All right, so maybe I did. But I was eighteen. You say a lot of stupid things at that age. If I recall, I hated broccoli and jazz, too. Both of which I've come to love over the years."

"So now you love children?"

"I didn't say that. Why are you being difficult?"

"Sorry," she said, realizing he was right. "The family isn't crazy about the idea of me taking on single parenthood, and I'm a little touchy on the subject."

That wasn't the only reason, but she wasn't going to tell him about the panic that had hit her ten years ago when she'd discovered she was pregnant. Although they'd used protection, the possibility that David might think she had deliberately allowed herself to get pregnant had scared her to death. Then, of course, it had become a moot point once the fight had begun.

David was still staring at her. She scanned the sky with one hand against her brow, though she couldn't honestly say she saw a thing. "We really ought to go."

Before she could stand, he held up his hands, offering the flower wreath. "Hold on. Let's see how this fits."

She ducked her head so that he could place the garland gently on her hair. The sweet, earthy scent of the blossoms was sharp in her nostrils, and against her forehead she felt its tickling weight. With a lazy stretch of his arm, David captured a curl at the side of her face, tucking it behind her ear with one finger.

The look in his eyes set her blood hammering.

"You don't look like a mom. You look like a fairy princess." There was a husky roughness in his voice that threatened to set off lightning currents of arousal within her if she didn't pay attention. For just a second, the meadow felt like a separate little island, isolated from time.

To break that spell, she pulled a nearby aster and placed it absently behind her ear.

David shook his head. "Wrong ear, I think. Placing a flower behind that one means you're married."

Reacting almost on autopilot, Addy slipped the flower behind her other ear.

He gave her a look that said she was hopeless. "That ear means you're single and still looking. But it sounds like you're not really *that,* either."

Thank God for the steadying hand of common sense. She plucked the aster from her hair. Her handling had left the fragile petals wilted and forlorn-looking.

She lifted his hand and dropped the wildflower into his open palm. "*This* way says that it's really none of your business."

CHAPTER SIX

FOR DAVID, AFTER THAT less-than-satisfying interlude with Addy in the meadow, the day steadily worsened.

Two hours away from their lunch stop he realized that he'd left his cellular phone behind. His office would be going crazy by now, trying to reach him. The phone was probably ringing frantically among the wildflowers, scaring the hell out of some jackrabbit.

It was permanently lost to him, and to his irritation, both Gran and Addy actually seemed pleased.

The hiking station was closed—according to the small sign on the door—due to illness. No ice for their cold drinks and perishables until the following day, when they could detour for a stop at another campground. It also meant no phone call could be made to David's office to let them know why he was suddenly incommunicado.

He spent most of the afternoon trying not to worry about that and ended up thinking about Addy instead. He tried to imagine her sleek curves distended by pregnancy and couldn't come up with the picture in his head. He tried to envision her married to a man like Brandon O'Dell, part of some loveless, comfortable agreement, and couldn't do that, either. If there was ever a woman who had been meant for grand passion, that woman was Addy. At least she had been ten years ago. Finally David gave up trying to think about *anything* and just settled for keeping Joe's head up from the grass.

Toward sundown it clouded up, threatening rain. Addy cast a worried glance skyward and picked up the pace.

They reached a pile of boulders that had been part of some long-ago rock slide. Addy jumped off Sheba and had just begun withdrawing slickers and waterproof tarps from Bounder's pack when the first fat drops of rain fell.

She pointed toward a rugged outcropping set into the cliff wall. "Take your grandmother up to that ledge. It's big enough for the three of us, and we can spend the night there."

"What about you?" David asked as he helped Gran from her saddle.

"I want to cover our stuff so it doesn't get wet." Thunder boomed, and Clover jumped nervously in front of her. "Go on! A little rain won't hurt me, but I don't want Geneva to get soaked."

After throwing a slicker around Gran's shoulders, David took a firm grip on her hand and headed toward the rocky ledge. By the time they reached the overhang his grandmother was out of breath, but at least she was dry.

"You all right?" he asked. His words bounced eerily among the shadowy rocks.

"Never better." Thunder crashed again, and she cast a worried glance toward the cliff opening. "Oh, poor Addy. She'll be drenched."

David took a quick glance around the wide ledge. It was dusty but habitable, with no significant deep, dark crevices that could harbor wild animals. The charred remains of a campfire sat in the center of the stone floor.

"Sit down and catch your breath," he told her. "I suppose it would be less than gentlemanly of me to stay up here and let our trail boss do what she gets paid for."

"It certainly would, dear. And besides, Addy isn't getting paid for this trip. She volunteered to take me."

That news surprised him. Plunging his arms into one of the slickers, he set off in a splashing run back down the trail.

He found Addy struggling to keep the wind from snatching one edge of the tarpaulin off Injun Joe's saddle. Wordlessly he rushed to the other side of the gelding, snapped the material taut and tucked it under the saddle blanket. All of the animals were tied securely to a fallen tree. Their ears twitched back and forth, but they seemed remarkably calm.

"Everything's covered," he shouted at Addy over the rain. "Let's get out of this!"

He grabbed her hand and pulled her after him. The path to the cliffside ledge was running with water. The ground was so hard-packed that not even the pounding raindrops could penetrate it.

They reached the dim, cool outcropping, soaked in spite of their rain gear, their lungs hitching for air. Gran had already begun the search for dry firewood.

Like a wet dog, David shook out of the slicker and tossed his head to rid his hair of excess water. His shirt was plastered to his body like a second skin, and his jeans felt heavy and unpleasant against his legs.

He looked at Addy, who had removed her slicker, too. Her hair hung in wet strands around her face, and her cheeks were bright with color.

Something else he noticed with a flicker of surprised pleasure: she wasn't wearing a bra. Yep, definitely not part of the wardrobe today.

Find something to do, McKay. Quickly.

It took four attempts to get a fire going, but it brightened them all considerably. The rocks warmed, and David's and Addy's clothing began to steam dry right on their bodies. Beyond the ledge, the rain was letting up, but it was clear that sleeping in this shallow cave would have to do tonight.

Gran was examining the sandstone walls, which were notched with crude markings and striated different colors from thousands of years of mineral deposits. "How did you know this place was here?" she asked.

"I ran across it a few years ago when I came out here with a—" Addy stopped. "With a friend."

Not him, David thought. He'd have remembered. So who *had* she been here with? O'Dell? And what did it matter anyway?

He watched her pull the front of her shirt away from her body so the heat could warm her flesh. The glow from the fire seemed to highlight the dark areolae of her... *Don't go there,* he told himself. Swallowing hard, he turned away to pretend an interest in their surroundings.

"Do you suppose some ancient Indian tribe once sought refuge here?" Gran asked.

Addy was preoccupied with squeezing water out of her hair, and as the drops fell onto the stones around the fire, they sizzled and danced. "Probably. This area is pitted with quite a few cliff dwellings of the Sinaguans. If you look hard enough, it wouldn't surprise me if you could make out specific symbols."

"Do you really think so?" Gran asked enthusiastically. "David, did you hear that? Isn't that exciting?"

"Uh-huh. I think I've found one already." Cocking his head to one side and squinting hard, he read, "'Curtis loves Mitzi forever. Go Blue Devils.'" He straightened, tossing a lazy grin in the direction of both women. "Those crazy, fun-loving Sinaguans."

Neither his grandmother nor Addy seemed to have a sense of humor anymore. They just frowned at him.

After the rain stopped they set up a cozy if somewhat primitive campsite. Since it would be impossible to pound tent stakes into solid rock, they'd have to settle for blankets and sleeping bags around the fire.

Gran had designated herself keeper of the flame, feeding logs into the fire so that no corner of the cave remained in darkness. As they moved back and forth around the fire, their elongated shadows leaped and danced on the walls of the cliff, as though prehistoric paintings had come to life and joined them.

They ate sandwiches and the remainder of the potato salad before the last bit of ice gave out. Addy brewed coffee in a battered pot that reminded him of one of the props from the last Western he'd produced, then surprised them with homemade peach cobbler for dessert. They warmed it in a pan set among the fire's ashes. The entire cave smelled of vanilla and cinnamon.

Full and satisfied, they drifted away to their own diversions. Gran sat with her sketch pad on her lap and colored pencils methodically laid out in colorful rows. David decided to pass time by examining the cliff walls to see if he could separate modern graffiti from ancient markings.

It wasn't easy. Crouching only inches away from the stone, his fingers rubbing away the grit and ruin of ages, he still couldn't make head or tails of most of it.

"Having any luck?" Addy asked, suddenly beside him.

He shook his head. "Not unless you're willing to believe that one of the early cliff dwellers was named Malibu Jack."

Her finger traced the lines of a bit of recent

commentary—the image of a heart linking two young romantics together. With a regretful sigh she said, "Isn't it a shame? The Sinaguans were here centuries ago, and in only a few years we've managed to obliterate almost all signs of them."

"I do hope the Devil's Smile has remained the way I remember it," Gran spoke up.

David snorted. "More likely there'll be a subdivision sitting smack-dab in the middle of it."

"Oh, David, don't say that." His grandmother set her pad down and gave him a pointed look. "Why aren't you working on that computer of yours?"

"The light's too fickle in here to make it worth bothering with tonight," he said.

The truth was, he was enjoying his search for evidence of early habitation. The ledge was adequate protection, but it was also spooky as hell, reminding him of trips he'd taken with Gran and Grampa Herb to places like Black Canyon of the Gunnison and Mesa Verde.

He'd forgotten how his stomach could clench with fear at the sight of ancient burial pits. Or pitch with excitement when he dug in the dirt and found the tiny skull of a prehistoric horse—which he knew in his heart was just the skeleton of some poor, unfortunate mouse but sure *looked* a lot like the picture of eohippus in the archeology book he'd gotten for Christmas.

In Los Angeles there weren't many occasions for that kind of exhilaration to hit you. Unless you were able to get a cab on a rainy night. Or the maître d' at an exclusive restaurant showed you to the best table without your having to tip him a fortune. Reasons for delight just got measured in different ways, he supposed.

Gran withdrew her camcorder from her satchel and filmed them all. It had been years since David had manned a camera, but night shoots were tricky, and he couldn't help pointing out ways to make her shots more interesting, less static.

Eventually he filmed a few frames himself, though the camcorder felt strange in his hands.

His father had been the photographer in the family, teaching David at an early age how to find his way around any kind of camera.

At home there had been a closet full of home movies and old photographs, seemingly every tiny detail of the McKay family recorded. After his parents had died and those memories had been boxed up and moved to his grandparents' basement, it took years for David to be able to look at any of that again. It was just too painful.

But as a teenager, he'd loved capturing his own *new* memories and he'd been drawn to documentaries when Grampa Herb had taken him to a film festival in Steamboat Springs. From that moment on, he hadn't wanted to do anything else. And when the film crew had come to Broken Yoke to make that Western, he'd done everything he could to ingratiate himself with the cast and crew. It had worked. Better than he had ever hoped it would. Only, somewhere along the way he'd gotten sidetracked by all the trappings of Hollywood.

The evening hours wore away. The fire burned down, still warm and comforting as the flames stretched toward the soot-black-ened rock ceiling.

Addy, crouched in a far corner, motioned

to David. "Take a look at this," she said, pointing to the cliff wall.

On the sandstone, no more than waist-high, lay a cluster of crude figures scratched into the rock. A snake, a man and gradually shrinking circles that could have represented the sun.

"What do you think? Is it the real thing?"

The likelihood of pictographs hundreds of years old remaining undisturbed by visitors to this area was infinitesimal. Yet, oddly, there was no modern-day graffiti anywhere near it.

"I don't know," he said with a grimace. "They could have been carved there last week by some pimply-faced kid from Poughkeepsie."

"Or they could have been put there by a Sinaguan who wanted to leave some trace of his people for future generations," she countered. She kicked at the stones that lay in front of her on the uneven floor. "These rocks have only recently fallen away. The markings could have been hidden until then. That's possible, isn't it?"

"Addy, I..."

He could see in her eyes how badly she wanted to believe that. Maybe he wasn't the only one who remembered what it was like to shape fantasies out of the meanest clay of reality. So who was he to say what was possible and what wasn't?

"Could be. Better to be hidden forever than destroyed."

"Exactly," she agreed, obviously warming to the idea. "That probably explains why I never noticed them before when I stopped here."

"So what do you want to do about them now? Not a particularly significant find, I'm afraid."

"No. I suppose not," she said, resting her chin on her palm. He was struck by the sudden reminder that she had one of the most captivating pouts he'd ever seen on a woman. She turned her head to look at him, her features full of delighted mischief. "We could pile the rocks back up the wall and hope that no one ever finds them again. I like the idea of knowing they're here, safe and undisturbed, but just our little secret. Would that be too selfish?"

"Why? Just because we don't want to

come back here to find the name of Malibu Jack's latest love interest scribbled over them?"

She gave him an odd look. "*Will* you ever come back here?"

He frowned. "I was speaking figuratively."

Quickly he began gathering loose stones. In wordless agreement, Addy joined him. Together they heaped rocks against the wall. The haphazard arrangement had to look natural.

Finally they stood back and observed their handiwork.

Addy dusted her hands together. "I feel like we just buried the treasure of Sierra Madre."

David gave her an amused look. "If the treasure of Sierra Madre was behind all that, I'd be tearing it down, not covering it up."

"Always so practical."

"Almost always," he agreed, wondering if she had even a clue of how *unpractical* his behavior had been of late.

In another few minutes Gran wandered off to the lip of the overhang to stargaze. Addy settled by the fire. David lay on top of his sleeping bag on his back, hands clasped behind his head, watching the dying flames play shadow games on the rocks. Thinking.

His mind replayed all the strange moments that made up one more day on this bizarre mission of Gran's.

Getting soaked—that was annoying. Losing the cell phone—that was even *more* annoying. He shifted his hips a little in discomfort. Having to sleep in new jeans—jeez, didn't that make him a candidate for sainthood?

Without moving his body, he turned his head. Addy seemed absorbed in the fire. Her hair lay loose against her back, like a flow of ink.

He thought of how sweetly enchanted she'd looked just a while ago, proposing her theories about those pathetic scratchings on the cave wall. The pleasure in her eyes as they'd finished restacking the stones. Most of all, how badly he'd wanted to kiss her.

David heard her sigh, but she didn't move a muscle. He scowled. He might have asked what she was thinking, but he wasn't sure he wanted to know.

Instead he went back to staring vacantly at the rock ceiling. He wasn't about to let his carefully planned life disintegrate into a bunch of lustful, intoxicating notions about a woman who had once accused him of some pretty ridiculous things.

He just needed to get through the next week and a half. Then he'd be back in Los Angeles. Back in the rat race that his life had become. Once he put the insanity of this trip behind him, everything would return to normal.

ADDY REALLY ENJOYED a campfire. The smell of the wood smoke. The crackle of flames. The way sparks seemed like fireflies against the night sky.

But right now she barely noticed that it had become no more than a red, hissing ring of burned logs.

Her slitted gaze kept straying back to the long, imposing shape that was David McKay lying on top of his sleeping bag. Strong thighs. Narrow hips. Flat stomach. The outline of muscle and easy strength was there, even in the ruddy light, and she experienced the same mortifying surge of heat she'd always felt whenever she looked at him.

He was staring up at the ceiling as though he were sunbathing on the Riviera, hands pinioned under his head. He seemed lost in concentration.

What was he thinking?

But of course, she knew the answer to that. He must really hate being here. He probably couldn't wait to get back to Los Angeles, where he thought he belonged.

Did he find it difficult to be in her company? Sometimes it almost seemed like the old days, as though ten years had disappeared and dropped them just where they'd left off. It was hard not to remember the good times. The day David had taught her how to play poker, the summer nights they'd spent on Lightning Lake, pretending an interest in the stars but finding so many excuses to touch one another.

But then he'd say something or do something that would trip a memory—a bad one—and she found herself eager to get away from him, reminded that you can't put the past behind you just like that. Could you?

When it came to David McKay, she thought she had built a firewall around those memories, but sometimes…

She'd never told him about the baby, but now she wondered what he would have said. Or done. How differently might things have turned out if she'd stopped him cold with that news.

Even back then David had been unhappy living in a small town like Broken Yoke. He'd probably made the decision to leave long before their child had been conceived. So would knowing her circumstances have changed anything? Probably not.

And once he'd gone, she couldn't have run after him. His life had taken a new path, a career most people would envy. Not the one he'd told Addy he wanted but a successful one nonetheless.

Whether she should go to Los Angeles to tell him about the baby had become a nonissue anyway. Just days after he'd left, she'd miscarried. Just like that, she wasn't pregnant anymore.

In spite of her initial fears about her situation, she'd been bereft. And even though she was still furious with David, she just couldn't tell him. Maybe it was different for men, but she couldn't imagine hurting anyone the way she hurt. Not even the man who had broken her heart.

Once he'd moved to Hollywood, sometimes she'd see David pictured with the up-and-comers, people whose every move was followed by the press. She knew he'd been hired to work for a production company, that his talents had been quickly spotted and encouraged. But did he have regrets at all about what had happened between them?

"David?" she called out softly.

"Hmm?"

"Can I ask you a question?"

He didn't turn his head toward her, just kept his eyes on the rocks above. But she saw him nod.

Addy straightened. "After you left Broken Yoke, was there ever a time when you were sorry you'd left?"

He turned his head, trying to meet her gaze in the flickering light. "I was eighteen, Addy. I was starstruck and stunned to have some of the film crew think I had a chance in Hollywood. They believed in me."

She looked at him. "Are you saying that I didn't?"

"I'm saying that they could answer a lot of questions I had about filmmaking and they were willing to. Leaving Broken Yoke..." He flicked a glance toward his grandmother, who was well out of earshot. "Leaving Gran and Grampa Herb...and you...wasn't something I wanted to do, but frankly, at that time in my life, it seemed like a price worth paying. I just never thought it would be permanent. I thought you would..."

He let the rest of that slip away, and neither of them said a word for a long time. A return to safer waters seemed in order. But where was that?

She thought about the way he'd so generously played along with her about the pictographs. The diamond mine of information he'd dredged up about ancient findings and then shared with her. Never in a stuffy, know-it-all kind of way, but fun, inventive. He'd always had such an inquisitive mind.

But those stones had been heavy, the

work tiresome and dirty. Why had David been so indulgent?

She bit her lip, trying to come up with reasons and failing. Finally, unable to stop herself, she called out softly again into the hush of their surroundings, "David?"

"Now what?" he said without looking at her.

"Those markings on the cliff wall weren't really ancient, you know."

His head turned toward her then, and in the fire's fading light she could see the gleam of his eyes trying to find hers. "I know," he returned in a voice that offered a smile.

"I…" She wet her lips. "It was kind of you to humor me that way."

His long silence had an effect on her she could not have foreseen. In spite of the distance, Addy felt as though a warm current was running between them. She thought she could breathe in his nearness like a flower's, could feel his fingers in her hair. The cave had become dark and intimate, and yet the air seemed to throb with tension.

It was frightening to think how completely they could reconnect. She and David were living such different lives now, and there was simply no point in letting this desperate undertow of desire tug at her. No point at all.

Addy gathered her defenses. "David…"

"I'm going to get Gran. It's time we all got some sleep."

The flurry of words beating loud wings within her dropped back into silence as David rose. There wasn't any need for them. Somehow he had guessed her thoughts and instinctively adopted them. She should have been glad that he was making it so easy for her. That sudden mad flush of attraction between them just a moment ago wasn't going to be acted on. Perhaps it would even be ignored.

Yes, that was definitely the right way to handle it. Ignore it and it would go away.

She felt better already.

CHAPTER SEVEN

GENEVA SCOWLED DOWN at the phone receiver. "Don't you yell at me, Sam D'Angelo. I'm doing the best I can."

"I apologize," Sam said in a slightly calmer voice. "But, damn it, you have to do something!"

"What? They're like oil and water. If he says it looks like rain, she says it won't. If she thinks it's time to stop for lunch, he thinks we should ride a half hour longer. I could shake them both."

"Why are they fighting?"

"They aren't fighting exactly. They're just…edgy."

"What about David's cell phone and computer? Did you find a way to neutralize them?"

Geneva couldn't help a little laugh. "You

sound like a secret agent when you talk like that."

She could tell Sam wasn't in the proper mood to appreciate that comment. "Well did you?" he asked.

"I didn't have to. He accidentally left his cell phone at one of the stops we made, and lately he hasn't seemed all that determined to work on his computer."

"That sounds promising. Maybe because he's more interested in what Addy's up to?"

"Maybe," Geneva acknowledged. "But so far this trip is definitely not working out the way we planned."

"Give me a minute. I'm thinking."

Geneva stood at the pay phone along the side of the building and kept a close eye out for Addy or David. They had finally arrived at a small complex consisting of a campground, restaurant/bar, service station and convenience store. Miles from the nearest town, it was the kind of place that struggled up out of the dust to find a toehold on a road map and could just as quickly and easily disappear. Still, the grounds were well kept, the customer bathrooms were clean and the restaurant/bar—Clementine's—looked... homey.

Both Addy and David were in the convenience store. The minute they had ridden up to the picnic area, David had headed for this line of battered pay phones. Addy had shaken her head, pulled a list out of her pocket and gone to get supplies.

Now, while David was trying to find out if there was Internet access anywhere close by, Geneva was pretending to be on the phone with her friend Polly, babysitter to Geneva's houseplants.

Sam was still silent on the other end, and the fact that he hadn't come up with an idea yet made Geneva feel slightly vindicated. It wasn't easy to get two stubborn people to see eye to eye. Especially about each other.

For a while they had seemed to be getting along splendidly, laughing and talking together. Geneva wasn't so ancient that she couldn't interpret those occasional looks and gestures that surreptitiously suggested sexual attraction.

But all that had ceased abruptly two days ago—the morning after they'd spent the night in the shallow cave. Everything since seemed to have grown out of that night.

Oh, they were polite to each other, but the reticence had come back in David, so that in his walled face not a muscle stirred. And Addy was too quiet and guarded, so introspective that she appeared a long way off, like a vanishing ghost.

Something had destroyed the budding harmony between them.

"I can't talk right now," Sam said suddenly. "Nick's coming."

"But what—"

"Improvise!"

"You're not helping," Geneva complained, but the line had already gone dead.

Annoyed, she placed the receiver back in its cradle, then walked over to the picnic tables and sat down. She pulled the toiletry bag containing the box of her husband's ashes onto her lap. Through the canvas her worn fingers caressed the intricate scrollwork on the lid. She wished Herbert were here. He would have known how to fix this.

"What can I do, Herbert?" she murmured aloud. A soft breeze played against her lined cheek, as though it sensed her frustration and sought to soothe. "Since Sam and I seem to be ridiculously short on inspiration, a little help from you certainly wouldn't go amiss. Are you listening, dear?"

The leaves on the ground around the picnic table moved in a dusty dance along the hard-packed dirt road. With a brooding sigh, Geneva listened to the rhythmic creaking of the restaurant's rusting sign as it swung back and forth on its hinges.

She straightened suddenly.

Behind the campground office, a few small redwood cabins lay in a semicircle of Douglas firs. She glanced back at the restaurant, narrowing her eyes to read the faded words above the door. Great Food, Great Times. Home Of The World's Best Chili. Try Us!

"Yes. I believe we must," Geneva said. "Thank you, Herbert."

Addy returned and began adjusting the packs on the mules. David joined them moments later.

"Did you reach your office, dear?" Geneva asked.

He placed one foot on the picnic bench,

using his Stetson to beat the dust out of his jeans. "Yes. Amazingly, everything is fine. When Rob—my assistant—couldn't get in touch with me, he decided to run with the responsibility. And he's done just great. I may have to give him a raise when I get back."

Addy spoke from over Sheba's saddle. "You mean Hollywood didn't close its doors while you've been gone?"

David said nothing. This close, Geneva witnessed the sudden tense pull along his jawline. "Ready for lunch, Gran?" he asked.

Geneva didn't like the dangerous calm in his voice. Oh, dear. In fractious moods, the both of them. She couldn't allow their remoteness to escalate into hostility.

She sighed heavily and let her lips form a tentative smile. "I suppose so. Though I'm really not very hungry."

"You should be," David said, then tossed a pointed look at Addy. "Breakfast wouldn't have fed a family of mice."

The younger woman slapped Sheba's rump out of her way and came to join them, clearly rankled. "I should have our supplies replenished soon," she said, looking as though she had something else she wanted to say but refusing to give in to the impulse. "We can eat lunch and be back on the trail in about an hour."

Feeling more certain that what she was about to do was wise, Geneva said in a weak, scattered voice, "The trail... Oh, yes, I suppose we must, mustn't we?"

David's head turned immediately, a frown descending on his dark brow. She felt his full attention swing alertly into focus. "Gran, are you all right?"

"Yes, of course..."

Addy hastened to her side, and Geneva experienced a little twinge of guilt for the look of worry she saw in the young woman's eyes. "Geneva, what is it?"

She clutched her hands in front of her, then twisted them together uncertainly. "Well, to tell you the truth, I *am* a little tired. The days are catching up with me." She sat up straighter, plastering a fake smile on her face. "But I'll be fine. Really. Shall we eat here?"

David had come around the table now, too, sitting on her other side, until she felt almost smothered by these loving guardians.

Gently he swiped a stray wisp of gray hair away from her cheek. "Gran, listen to me. If you're too worn out, if you're ready to give up on this trip, we can—"

"Oh, no!" she said in a quick explosion of speech. Then she added more softly, "It's nothing like that. I'm just a spoiled old woman who's discovered that she misses the luxury of a hot bath and a good home-cooked meal." She turned toward Addy. "Not that you haven't done a wonderful job so far, Addy."

She allowed the words to settle. The three of them sat quietly for a moment. Addy was frowning at her in an odd, calculating way that made Geneva nervous. David looked worried, as though he suspected she was hiding the truth about her state of exhaustion.

"We could have lunch at the restaurant," Addy suggested at last.

Geneva cleared her throat. "I was thinking…dinner. I would so love to have a nice juicy steak."

Addy shook her head. "You know you can't have too much red meat. It's not good for you."

"Whatever you want, Gran," David overruled her.

Geneva smiled and lifted a spindly finger. "And do you suppose those little cabins over there are for rent? Wouldn't it be lovely to take a hot bath and sleep in a real bed tonight?"

She knew she could count on David not to waste time. He took one look at the cabins and rose immediately to carry out her wishes. "We can use the break. I'll see what can be arranged." He glanced at Addy. "Would you have a problem with that?"

"No."

He nodded shortly. "Just rest, Gran. I'll be right back."

The two women watched him stride off for the campground office.

Now if only Addy would stop making her so uncomfortable. She hadn't taken her eyes off Geneva since the moment she'd sat down, and Geneva was sure her neck and cheeks were flaming with guilt.

"Geneva, what's going on in that head of yours?"

Geneva found sudden interest in crude initials carved into the redwood table and tried to keep her face a picture of bewilderment. "I don't know what you mean, dear. I just thought a change might do us all some good." Before Addy could grill her further, she rose to her feet. "I really must visit the ladies' room."

"I thought you did already," Addy said, her suspicion evident.

"You know how it is when you get older," Geneva replied mysteriously and hustled away.

When she returned, David said he had rented two of the cabins for the night.

"Hope you ladies won't mind sharing," he told them. "The manager said he had only two right now that were 'rentable.' I didn't want to ask what that meant exactly."

With the matter settled, David insisted that Geneva spend the afternoon resting. She chafed at being forced to remain inside but tried to summon up a look of appreciative relief for David's benefit. "What about the two of you?" she asked fretfully.

"I've got at least a dozen phone calls to make," David told her. "And I've managed to snag some Internet time from the campground owner."

"I may do some laundry," Addy threw in. "Or give the animals a good rubdown. This place caters to campers who trailer their horses to some of the local rodeos, so they have what I need." She hefted her knapsack over her shoulder. "After that, I intend to take your suggestion. A nice hot soak in a real bathtub."

That was not precisely what Geneva had hoped for—the two of them going their separate ways again—but it was a start. And she still had the evening to work out something clever.

Just what that would be... Well, maybe she'd see if she could summon up Herbert's spirit again. He was certainly more helpful than that wretched Sam D'Angelo.

AT PROMPTLY SIX-THIRTY they met in front of the cabins and walked across the dirt road to Clementine's. Addy noticed that there were only a few cars pulled haphazardly in front, mostly pickup trucks. When they entered, they had to stand a few moments to let their eyes adjust, the interior was that dim compared to the fading sunset outside.

Gran seemed to warm to the place immediately. "Oh, isn't this charming, David? Such ambience."

His gaze swept over the restaurant. "Since when did *ambience* become another word for *clutter?*"

The place was pretty much what Addy had expected. Lots of cattle horns and antlers everywhere, nostalgic signs and an odd collection of Elvis memorabilia decorating one wall. Overhead, a couple of toy trains ran along a track that crisscrossed the restaurant. An old-fashioned jukebox belted out a sad song about killing the man who stole his woman.

Cowboy chic without the chic part.

Oh, I'll bet David's wishing someone would beam him back to Los Angeles right now.

Addy tossed him an amused look. "Not exactly one of those fancy places on Rodeo Drive, is it?"

He gave her a mechanical smile. "No, but Gran's right. It still beats campfire ashes in your food and not enough ice in your glass."

Exasperated, Addy turned back around.

"Don't pay any attention to him," Geneva told her. "You know he's always a bear when he's hungry."

A woman in jeans and a tank top came to

greet them. She led them directly across the empty wooden dance floor to a round table barely big enough for the three of them, plopped plastic menus in front of their faces and threatened to return in a few minutes.

Gran lifted her head to watch the toy train make a noisy pass over their table. "Isn't that interesting? The owner must collect them."

"Uh-huh," David replied, holding his fork up to the meager light to inspect it.

Addy hid a smile behind her menu. She didn't know what Geneva had up her sleeve, but she seemed determined to pull David into the middle of it. Why was he behaving like such a pill?

And why did he have to look so sexy tonight?

One dark lock had fallen over his forehead, catching every gleam of the restaurant's mood lighting, and the top buttons of his blue shirt were open just enough to reveal a crisp matting of equally dark chest hair. It was a darned good thing she'd made up her mind two days ago not to pay much attention to that sort of stimulus.

The waitress came back, pencil poised to take drink orders. Geneva and Addy requested iced tea. David asked for some odd variety of gin, and the woman looked at him as if he'd just dropped in off a distant planet.

"We got beer," she said flatly. "And a few call brands."

"Beer's fine. What kind do you have?"

"Cold."

David took a long moment to look up at her. "Then…" he said slowly, "I guess that would be my choice."

"Right you are."

Before she could slip away, he stopped her. "Could we also have ice water?"

"All three of you?" the woman asked with a quick frown.

"I'm afraid so."

She nodded and trotted away. Utter silence descended on the table. David gazed up at the ceiling as though patience would be delivered by one of the toy trains. Geneva pleated her napkin over and over, and Addy was trying hard not to laugh.

She lost all hope when Geneva, with a twinkle in her eye, leaned across her menu to say, "For David's sake, I do hope they put lots of ice in the glasses."

Addy nodded and replied in mock severity, "He likes his cold things cold and his hot things hot, you know?"

David slapped his menu on the table and gave them both a sour glance. "There's nothing wrong with liking things a certain way," he said succinctly. "And the fact that she glared at us as though we were camels stocking up for a trek across the Sahara will certainly be reflected in her tip. The service industry has gotten way too—where are you going?" he asked as his grandmother began to rise from the table.

"The ladies' room."

"I'll come with you," Addy offered.

"Oh, no, you mustn't!" the old woman said quickly. Then in an agonized whisper she added, "Bashful-kidney syndrome."

Settling in her chair, Addy watched Geneva make her way across the dance floor. They fell back into silence once more as David seemed absorbed in reading the menu. Addy caught sight of the little train coming around again and counted the boxcars.

Finally, unable to contain her thoughts any longer, she leaned across the table.

"David, do you think there's anything strange about this?"

"Anything strange? I don't think there's anything *normal* about this place," he replied from behind his menu.

"I don't mean the restaurant. I mean the fact that your grandmother practically twisted our arms to get us to spend the night here."

"She said she was tired."

"Does she look tired to you?"

"No, but that could be a front. She's sneaky sometimes."

"Exactly. I think she's faking it."

He put down his menu. One dark eyebrow lifted. "Why?"

"I think she wanted us to stay here overnight, and pretending to need rest was one sure way to get us to do it."

He heaved an exaggerated sigh. "Again I ask, why?"

Now that she had his full attention, she wasn't going to sidestep voicing her suspicions, even if they were more than a little embarrassing. "While we were getting ready tonight, Geneva was as animated as a teenager going to the prom. She must have asked me three times if I'd brought anything more festive than this," Addy said, lifting the fabric of her blue-and-red-plaid blouse. "And she insisted that I wear my hair down. I could be wrong, but I think that old woman is matchmaking."

"Between the two of us?" David said with a scowl. "That's ridiculous. No way."

Addy fell back in her chair. "Well, thank you very much."

"I don't mean it that way," he amended with a look of indulgent patience. "I just mean that she knows our history. She knows that we have completely different lives. Besides, if she wanted to play Cupid, why would she pick now? And *here* of all places?"

"Because as pitiful as it is, this is still a more conducive atmosphere than the hard, dusty trail. No work required. We're all fairly relaxed." She lowered her glance to the table. Then, eyeing him cautiously, she added in a hushed voice, "I think she's hoping for something to…develop. At the very least, a truce between us."

His gaze held hers in a warm study. "I wasn't aware we were at war."

The waitress brought their drinks and water, setting them on the table without a word. When David told her they weren't quite ready to order dinner, she nodded curtly and disappeared.

Addy took a large swallow of tea and refused to backpedal now. She leaned forward again. "You have to admit it's been a little…tense the past couple of days."

David's head jerked slightly, and he gave her an odd look. "Considering our past, how could it be anything else?"

"Can't we just be friends for a little while?" she asked in disgust. "We've only got a week and a bit to go."

It seemed to take him a long time to decide how he wanted to answer that. With his head cocked to one side, he fingered his knife. Finally he said, "I'm not sure that would be wise."

"Fine. But if our irritation with one another is making your grandmother uncomfortable, it wouldn't hurt to *pretend* to get along for her sake, would it?"

"I suppose not. What would I have to do?"

"Well, for one thing, you can stop sounding like I've just asked you to clean out a sewer." She opened her napkin with an audible snap, then gave him a severe look. "You know, Brandon thinks I'm a fascinating conversationalist. In fact, a lot of men have found being in my company very enjoyable."

She watched his pliant smile reappear as he gazed at her with lazy curiosity. "Really? How many?"

"If you're not going to take this seriously…"

He held up one hand. "Okay, trail boss. You win," he conceded with a laugh and tipped his beer bottle in her direction as a salute. "Bosom buddies from this moment on."

She cleared her throat and added primly, "Figuratively speaking."

The smile twitched into a sexy wolfish grin that nearly took her breath away. "Of course."

CHAPTER EIGHT

WHETHER GENEVA WAS matchmaking or not, Addy was relieved when the woman returned and she was no longer alone with David. The waitress wandered back to take their order of steaks and baked potatoes. A few more people came in—not exactly a dinner rush—but enough to make the place livelier and drown out the sound of the trains chugging overhead. Or maybe they had just become used to it.

At the bar a couple of cowboys were boisterously involved in a contest to see who could flip a quarter off their nose into a shot glass. On the jukebox Patsy Cline was going crazy for falling in love.

The T-bones were good. The waitress kept the water and tea glasses full without having to be flagged down, and David seemed to discover a taste for the beer.

In spite of that, dinner was still uncomfortable. Geneva *was* matchmaking.

Throughout the meal she continually found ways to point out the similarities between what she referred to as "her two favorite people." She shared tales that were obviously designed to amuse and intrigue each of them about the other. Addy began to feel as though she was present at her own memorial service. From the look of commiseration in David's eyes, she knew he felt the same.

She had to admit, Geneva's attempts were not entirely lost on her. The beer seemed to have mellowed David somewhat, and she glimpsed some of his old charm. He poked fun at himself and laughed often.

Every so often Geneva would say something outrageously boastful about one of them, and his gaze would connect with Addy's. It was a powerful sensation—that ephemeral harmony—and, blinded momentarily by pure pleasure, she began to imagine that the real world had vanished. That there was nothing beyond this sweet, silent communion between them.

The waitress took away their dinner plates and offered coffee. David ordered another beer.

"Isn't that a lovely song?" Geneva remarked as the jukebox began to play the same Patsy Cline tune again.

"Somebody sure thinks so," David remarked, turning in his chair to find out who was plugging quarters into the machine. "That's about the sixth time we've heard it."

Addy patted her lips and folded her napkin on the table. "I think it's our waitress. A while back she stood there for five minutes shoving in one quarter after another."

They sat for a long moment listening to the music. A few couples moved onto the dance floor. The two cowboys at the bar had given up their competition and watched the room with nonchalant fingers hooked around the tops of their beer bottles.

"It's so nice to see young people slow dancing," Geneva said with a soft sigh. "No one does that anymore."

David tossed his napkin away and stood, offering his hand. "Gran, would you like to dance?"

"Oh, goodness, no," the old woman

replied quickly. "But don't let the music go to waste. Why don't you and Addy...?"

He raised an inquiring eyebrow across the table. "Trail boss?"

Surprised by how easily he surrendered to his grandmother's ploy, Addy could only nod agreement.

He took her hand and led her onto the dance floor, sliding an arm around her waist and bringing their entwined fingers to his chest. She was close to him as she hadn't been in years. Her heart bucked in her breast, and she thought despondently that it might have been a huge mistake to try to bridge the vast canyon of differences between them. Even temporarily. Even for the sake of someone as dear as Geneva.

Keep it light, Adriana, she lectured herself, trying to recoup her suddenly shaky courage. *David's not having a problem with this, and neither should you.*

His eyes were on her face. She turned to glance toward Geneva, who was watching from the sidelines with a ridiculously pleased smile. "You walked right into that one," she told him softly.

"I know," he said with a shrug. "So? How am I doing?"

"If you get any more agreeable tonight, I may be sick."

"You called the tune, lady. I'm just dancing to it."

That stung a little, and she snapped her head around to face him. "Is it really that hard? To be nice to me, I mean."

He gave her a lopsided grin. "No. In fact, you make it too damned easy." His tone was light and tender, and when she frowned at him, the hand around her waist tightened. "Smile," he commanded. "We're being watched."

She looked back at Geneva, who, without taking her eyes off them, was waving away the waitress's offer of more coffee. "She's relentless."

"The Mafia has more subtle methods than that old woman."

"I feel like a filly on the auction block."

"I guess that would make me a stud."

Addy eyed him again. "Are you drunk?"

"No. Are you?"

"Not drinking iced tea all evening."

"Should have had a few beers," he said in

a contented tone. "It's home brew and pretty potent. Gives everything a nice rosy glow."

"And a headache in the morning, no doubt."

His gaze traveled over her. "Some things are worth a little pain." He swung her into a sudden turn, and force of habit made her glance over her shoulder to make sure they wouldn't bump into anyone. "Relax, Addy," he told her. "I know where I'm going."

But I don't, she wanted to tell him and realized that the *something* beating in the roof of her mouth seemed to be her heart.

He pulled her even closer, so that she was aware of his strength and balance and command. He moved well, and she thought how nice it would be to nestle against him as he led her around the dimly lit dance floor. His cheek rested alongside hers, and she felt the warmth of his breath.

"Gran was right," he said softly, nuzzling her ear.

Nervous tingles began to play up Addy's spine. What took Patsy so long to finish that song? Honestly, why did country-western singers have to wring five syllables out of every word? "Right about what?"

"You should always wear your hair down." This was definitely turning into something that didn't feel "light" at all. *Pull yourself together. You're slipping.*

Desperately her mind searched for a safe topic of conversation. What had Geneva divulged over dinner? What nonsense had she read about him recently?

"David…"

"Mmm?"

"When you produced *Jet-Setter* in Italy, did you and Rex Hollister really share a night in your hotel room with four women?"

"No," he said without missing a step. "It was only three." When she straightened to look at him, he laughed. "I'm kidding. The only thing Rex Hollister and I shared on that film was the desire to make *Jet-Setter* a success. Which it was."

"I didn't see it."

He frowned at her. "It wasn't bad. And I did get to brush up on my Italian."

That surprised her even more. "You speak Italian?"

He nodded. "I can speak four languages. But after spending so much time way back when listening to your parents, I really fell in love with Italian. How's this? *Ti amo. Mi vuoi sposare?*"

In spite of her best effort, Addy felt a warm blush creep up her neck. *I love you. Will you marry me?* Even if she hadn't known Italian, the bold, smoldering look in David's eyes was too personal to be misunderstood.

But this was just nonsense and too much beer talking. Quickly Addy replied, *"Mai in vita mia." Never in my life.*

David laughed again. "I thought you might say that. Want to hear more?"

"No."

"I'm very good, *cara mia.* It's all in the way you roll your tongue."

Addy's breath stopped as a warm wetness slid along her ear. Moths fluttered in her stomach. They were playing far too dangerously. She jerked her head back. "Stop that!"

He stared at her with a smile so devastatingly charming it would have melted the inhibitions of a saint. "Don't stiffen up. I'm just pretending. Remember?"

Addy was thoroughly annoyed with him.

And herself. Really, she was pathetically helpless when it came to refusing this man. "Well, do your pretending with your tongue in your mouth, not my ear."

He seemed unperturbed. "You have no imagination."

"And *you* have too much."

"My curse, I'm afraid. Do you know, there have been times in Los Angeles when I could still picture us on Lightning Lake. That yellow bathing suit you kept falling out of because it was too big. Do you—" He looked back over his shoulder, and Addy realized that one of the cowboys from the bar was trying to cut in. "Sorry, pal," David said with affable regret in his voice. "The lady's dance card is full."

As David turned back to her, the man flashed him a sour glare, but he returned to his friend at the bar, who passed him a beer. She didn't like the way the men continued to stare.

"Now, where was I?" David said.

To avoid any potential trouble, both from the cowboys and David's unexpected walk down memory lane, Addy suddenly pulled away. "I think we've both had enough dancing for one night."

An audacious twinkle lay in the bright blue depths of David's eyes. "You're going to miss my tango. Don't you want to see what I can do with a rose between my teeth?"

"I don't think so," she said.

He led her back to their table, but they had no more settled into their seats before Geneva stood. "I think I'll return to the cabin," she said. When David made a motion toward the waitress, she added hastily, "Oh, please! Don't you two make an early night of it just because I'm getting sleepy. Besides, I ordered dessert."

"Gran," David said, rising, "we'll all call it a night. We can use the extra rest."

"But…" Geneva looked momentarily flustered.

"Actually some dessert might be nice," Addy chimed in, and when Geneva glanced her way, she winked at the old woman. She wasn't sure she hadn't just made the stupidest move of her life, but David's grandmother had been trying so hard to engineer the evening that Addy didn't have the heart to see her stumble at the finish line.

Besides, it wasn't as though there was

anything to worry about now that she and David weren't dancing together. And touching.

As though willing to be maneuvered one last time, David shrugged and took his grandmother's arm. "All right. We'll stay and have dessert. But I'm going to walk you back to the cabin."

"I'm perfectly capable of—"

"A lot of things," he finished for her. "Yes, I know. But I'm walking you back." He glanced at Addy. "Stay here. Order coffee. And don't eat my dessert."

She and Geneva wished each other goodnight, and David led his grandmother through the gloom of the restaurant and out the door. The waitress brought slices of mud pie, and Addy ordered David's coffee.

She sat with her chin on her hand and waited for his return, poking her fork through the cookie crust of her pie.

In spite of Geneva's manipulations, the evening had been fun. It had been nice to have her relationship with David return to the old ways. Before they'd mucked it up so completely.

Maybe…

What was she thinking? This was the man who had ditched her for Hollywood. This was the man who had broken her heart. She had too many plans for the future to risk everything now. So how could he be short-circuiting her willpower again?

You're in big trouble. Every time he looks at you that certain way, your bones turn to oatmeal.

Becoming aware of movement beside her, Addy looked up with a guilty start, expecting to find that David had witnessed her reverie. Instead the cowboy who had tried to cut in on the dance floor slid into David's empty seat.

THE FULL MOON PAINTED everything silver, lending this little oasis a glamour it couldn't boast in daylight. But Gran seemed disinclined to enjoy the quiet scenery. The door to the restaurant had no sooner closed behind them than David found himself having to take several ground-eating steps to catch up with his grandmother.

"Slow down," he said, delaying her with a

gentle touch along her arm. "We're not running a marathon."

"You'll want to get back to the restaurant."

"What for? Are you afraid I'll miss the one hundred and sixty-third time the little red caboose passes over our heads?"

Even in the pale moonlight he couldn't miss her peevish glance. "I *thought* you might want to get back to Addy."

After what he'd endured from his grandmother tonight, he couldn't resist the temptation to tease. "Why?" he asked placidly. "I've warned her not to eat my dessert."

She came to an abrupt halt and looked up at him with narrowed eyes. "Are you being deliberately obtuse?"

"You've lost your touch, Gran."

"Just what is that supposed to mean?"

He gave her a reproachful glance. "Do you remember the movie *Cleopatra,* when Cleopatra had herself sent to Caesar wrapped up in a rug? And they made this huge ceremony of unrolling it at the emperor's feet and out she popped?"

"Yes…"

One dark eyebrow lifted in amusement.

"Liz Taylor was delivered with less fuss and bother than the way you've been throwing Addy at me all evening."

"I've done no such thing!"

She started toward the campground cabins again, moving more quickly than he would have guessed she was able, but he wasn't going to let her off the hook so easily.

He matched his stride to hers. "Oh, yes, you have. As soon as I get back to Los Angeles I'm making a dentist appointment. I've had to swallow so much sweet stuff about Addy tonight that I'm sure I need cavities filled." He spread his hands in front of him and began ticking off his fingers. "She brings sick kids from the hospital up to the lodge. She knows how to repair a helicopter. She's on the committee that's trying to save the bighorn sheep in Alpine Glen. God, my teeth hurt!"

Gran stopped again, her mouth forming a protest before she even turned. "I don't see the harm in trying to get you to notice what a fine woman she's become."

"Who says I haven't noticed?"

"Oh. Well, I'm glad to know you're not completely beyond hope."

"I don't need you trying to resurrect something between the two of us that died long ago." For good measure, he added, "And I'm perfectly capable of attracting a woman on my own."

"Of course you are. I just want to be sure you attract the right one. You can't tell me that Addy isn't a considerable improvement over any of those women you meet in that decadent megalopolis you call home."

He laughed outright, then looping her arm in his, he led her along the gravel path. "How about letting me be the one to decide who's right and who's wrong for me?"

"I just want—"

He held up a forestalling hand. "I know what you want. But back off, will you?"

"Addy is perfect for you. She always has been."

He gave her a serious look. "Has it occurred to you that Addy might not be any more interested in this scheme of yours than I am? I've seen nothing in her attitude to indicate she's receptive to any of this, and she's got that O'Dell fellow salivating after her. Plus all this talk about wanting a baby as soon as possible."

"Plans can change. I tell you—"

"Put away your arrows, Cupid." David cut into any further campaigning on her part. They had reached the steps to the front porch of the cabin she shared with Addy. "I want you to behave from here on out."

"But—"

He shook his head at her. "It's time you and your bashful kidneys got to bed." He planted a kiss on her wrinkled cheek. "Good night."

With one last sullen look, she went into the cabin.

All the way back to Clementine's David told himself he should polish off the dessert Gran had ordered, swallow a quick cup of coffee and then set Addy at the door of her cabin without so much as a backward glance.

There was no purpose to be served in delaying the end of what had been a most unusual evening. They planned to make an early start in the morning. He could use a good night's sleep in a real bed instead of on the hard ground. And the beer had steadily taken its toll, leaving him feeling slightly fuzzy and reckless.

Which was why he knew, as surely as he knew his own name, that he wasn't going to listen to those inner voices urging him to call it a night. Instead he quickened his pace, tossing aside all logic in his eagerness to return to the restaurant.

Maybe what he'd told his grandmother was true. Maybe there wasn't a hope in hell that he and Addy could start something up again. But he couldn't pack it in yet. Not with Addy waiting for him, alone and beautiful and amiable. Not when there was still a drop or two to be wrung out of these moments with her.

His brain told him it was pointless. His brain made sense. But his body insisted on sending out entirely different messages.

Desire had ridden him hard the last two days, leaving him wide-eyed when he should have been asleep, irritated over trivialities and restless with so much wanting that he sometimes had to physically remove himself from her presence just to keep from embarrassing himself with a public display. So much for self-control.

With problems like that, could he have accompanied her back to her cabin, tipped his new Stetson to her and whispered a quick, impersonal good-night?

Not a chance.

He opened the door of the restaurant and wound his way back to their table. He slowed his approach when he realized that company had taken root across from Addy—one of the cowboys from the bar, the same one who had tried to cut in on their dance earlier.

He swore under his breath and stopped directly in front of them. "Sorry, friend," he said with a smile. "You're in my seat."

The man looked up at him, his expression conveying surly defiance. "I thought you'd paired off with the old broad."

David ignored the remark. Addy's eyes found his. She was toying with her dessert, but her gaze was hopeful and a little uneasy. "I was just explaining to this gentleman that you'd be right back."

"And here I am," David said, spreading his arms.

"Shouldn't leave such an attractive lady by herself, mister," came a voice from behind him, and David turned. The other cowboy had come to join his friend and perhaps lend support.

"You're absolutely right. How about we three fellows have a talk?"

Addy seemed clearly worried now and made a move to rise. "David…"

He stopped her with a firm hand on her shoulder. "It's all right, Addy. We're just going to discuss a couple of things over at the bar." David's smile encompassed both men. "Okay, guys?"

As though unsure of David's easygoing friendliness, the cowboys exchanged glances. Then, with a shrug, they followed in his wake as he headed toward the bar.

CHAPTER NINE

ADDY WATCHED THEM GO with a sense of impending doom. Those two cowboys had smelled strongly of beer, and Clementine's looked as if it had hosted more than its fair share of barroom brawls.

The three men talked a few minutes, with occasional glances in her direction. Her nerves ripped like silk every time one of them gestured broadly, expecting someone to throw a punch. David was tall and well-built, but if a fight broke out, it would still be two against one. The cowboys looked tough and rangy, like junkyard dogs eager to bite. Maybe she should try to find the manager of the restaurant, just in case.

But in the moment when she would have risen and done just that, David was returning to her table. The two cowboys hoisted themselves back onto their bar stools and nursed fresh beers, watching as he lowered himself into the chair across from her.

Without offering one word of explanation, David picked up his fork and cut into the pie. He took a sip of coffee, grimaced and set it back down. "Coffee's cold," he said.

Unable to contain her curiosity, Addy leaned across the table. "Well?"

"Well what?"

"Everything all right?"

"Sure. Why shouldn't it be?"

"I was afraid—a place like this…there's probably been more than one bar fight."

He tucked his chin and gave her an incredulous look. "I don't get involved in bar fights."

She slid a glance toward the cowboys. They were still giving them their full attention. "Maybe not. But those two look like *they* do."

He shot her a wide smile. "Were you worried about me? Think I was going to have to duke it out—two against one?"

"Two against two. You don't think I'd stand idly by and let them beat the stuffing out of you, do you?"

He slipped a forkful of mud pie into his mouth and chewed thoroughly before he cocked an egotistical eyebrow her way, armored in immaculate and pleased composure. "What makes you so sure I'd lose?"

She didn't know whether to be relieved or annoyed. He was acting strangely, covering something up, but she couldn't put her finger on what.

In a savage overtone she said, "All right. I can't stand it. How did you talk them into leaving us alone?"

"I'm a good negotiator. I do it all the time. And, as it turns out, they're just a couple of romantics."

"What does that mean?"

He pushed aside his empty dessert plate and leaned across the table so that their faces were only inches apart. His smile widened and he gave her a conspiratorial half wink. Softly he said, "I told them you were my girlfriend and that tonight I was trying to get up the courage to propose."

Whatever she had been expecting him to say, that certainly hadn't been it. Her jaw dropped. "What?"

"With guys like Pete and Fred, it's considered almost a requirement of the species that you show support to a fellow male when he's about to take the plunge. They gave me a few suggestions—none of which I think you'd appreciate or agree to—and sent me back over here with their best wishes."

She was hardly aware of the fact that he'd taken her cold hand in his. "I don't believe it."

"Don't frown, sweetheart. They'll think you turned me down." He lifted her fingers to his mouth, laying a few kisses across her knuckles. "Now smile like I just popped the question and nod your head."

She did as he asked, too stunned not to obey. His eyes, direct and piercing under lazy lids, sparkled with mischief.

"See? That wasn't so hard, was it?" His voice barely above a whisper, he added, "Pucker up, my intended. Time to seal this engagement with a kiss."

Before she could think or say another word, his hand reached across the table, his fingers slid beneath her hair to the back of her neck and he pulled her to him. His mouth closed over hers. She thought vaguely that she ought to be embarrassed, kissing in a public place, even one so seemingly uninhibited as Clementine's. But she found she liked the bold, heavy curve of his lips against hers and she waited for him to deepen it. It seemed as though his touch were a marauder whose grasp she could not escape. He tasted of chocolate and coffee. Rich and dark and sweet.

His mouth lifted from hers, though he still kept her pinned close with his hand behind her head. She felt his thumb rubbing warm circles just below her ear. His eyes wandered over her face, and in kind of a daze she watched his expressive mouth gather into another grin.

"Not bad," he said. "Good enough to convince those two lunkheads over there and *definitely* good enough to make me wish we'd gotten engaged sooner. I'm all yours, trail boss. Pick the date."

He glanced toward the cowboys and gave them a smile and the thumbs-up signal. They tipped their beer bottles at him in a salute and issued whooping sounds of triumph that made several heads turn in that direction.

She and David spent another few minutes looking appropriately love-struck. He paid the bill, bought the two fellows a round of drinks to say thanks and, before any further discussion could take place, ushered Addy out of the restaurant.

He didn't release her hand once they got outside. Side by side they walked back to the cabins under the pure white light of the moon, savoring the air's velvety mildness. Addy realized that, in spite of everything, she felt incredibly peaceful, protected.

She must have made some sound, perhaps a sigh of contentment, because David turned his head toward her, curiosity in his expression. "Thinking about whether it should be a big church wedding or an elopement?"

Sensitive nerve centers registered swift alarm. How could she tell him that her heart had begun to beat thickly just from his proximity? That the evening spent in his company was still bubbling inside her like champagne and she almost wished it would never end.

Embracing caution, she settled for a little white lie. "I was just thinking that you do nice work. First with Gran, then with those two baboons in the restaurant."

"You're a good sport, Addy. I was expecting a tongue-lashing once we got outside."

"Why? According to Geneva, you're the catch of the century."

"Aren't I, though?" he agreed in a self-mocking tone. Then he shook his head. "Lord, Gran hasn't embarrassed me that badly since the last time she spit-washed my face in front of friends."

They laughed together. It had a nice, companionable sound, and afterward even the silence itself seemed intimate.

"We had a little talk," David continued. "I think she'll lay off the both of us from now on."

Addy nodded and tried to appear suitably pleased. They mounted the three wide steps to the cabin porch, and she turned to face David. In the gentle glow of the outside light he looked so sexy, and she wished her heart would stop taking up an uncomfortably large portion of her chest.

"Well…" she began uncertainly, then stopped, disconcerted by the warmth in his smoky eyes.

In a reminiscent tone he remarked, "Standing on a front porch with a date—I haven't done this since I left Broken Yoke."

A date? Is that what tonight had been? Addy found her throat suddenly tight. "Not many front porches in the big city."

"Nope. Just doormen and cabbies who wish you wouldn't take so long to say good night and keep them waiting."

"I had a nice time tonight," she said, annoyed that she couldn't come up with anything more dazzling to say and mortified that even that had come out in a breathy little catch of sound.

"In spite of Gran's orchestrating?"

"Maybe even because of it," she said daringly.

She felt the doorknob pressing against her hip. David leaned closer, resting his forearm high against the wood beside her head, so that she could see the golden flecks of the porch light reflected in his pupils.

"We spent the entire evening pretending," she said softly. "If not for your grandmother's benefit, then for those two Neanderthals at the bar."

"Did we?" he asked, and their eyes met in a long look of complete understanding. "Sometimes it didn't feel that way."

His hand toyed with her hair as he let strands slip over and between his fingers. She stared at him, feeling inadequately equipped to play this game and wanting to anyway.

"No," she murmured. "Sometimes it didn't feel like we were pretending at all."

He lowered his head, taking her lips in a gentle way that brought a humiliatingly immediate response within her. Fire bloomed in the pit of Addy's stomach.

She felt caught between two worlds— equidistant from adventure and foolish regret—and decided in that moment to eliminate regret from her vocabulary. This wasn't the kiss he'd given her in the restaurant— quick and teasing. This was the real thing, and it felt too wonderful to be denied. She had simply ceased, at least temporarily, to care what overtook her.

When he drew away at last, she lifted a raw, questioning glance to him. Her chin lay captured between his fingers, and his thumb wandered the line of her jaw in a warm caress.

"What did that feel like?" he asked with casual, tender humor.

She heard herself say inadequately, "Nice. Like the real thing."

"That's because it was." His smile broadened as he absently stroked her cheek. "Addy, Addy. Are you sure you know what the hell you want? Do you look like this when Brandon O'Dell kisses you? You have so much to give a man. Just how big a sacrifice are you willing to make to get that baby?"

Addy stiffened, slamming the door shut on flickering desire. "I don't really want to talk about my relationship with Brandon with you. And nothing I have to do to have a baby in my life would be considered a sacrifice." She placed her hand on the doorknob of the cabin. "I wouldn't expect you to understand that."

Before he could reply and before Addy could turn the knob and slip inside, the door opened and Geneva peeked around it.

One hand was clutched at the neckline of

her robe. She looked pale and fretful. "I'm sorry to disturb you," she said. "But just a few minutes ago I did something very stupid. I'm afraid we might have to find a doctor."

THE DOCTOR THEY WERE lucky enough to find having dinner at Clementine's seemed bored and annoyed. Probably because a broken arm wasn't much of an emergency. And Geneva was not what anyone would call a cooperative patient.

They were all seated in the little cabin, letting the doctor's diagnosis sink in. Geneva spoke up, looking mulish in spite of her pale complexion.

"I don't see why I have to go to the hospital," she said to the doctor. "You said it looked like a simple fracture. Why can't you just tape it up securely until I can get it taken care of when we return home?"

The doctor looked surprised. "Mrs. McKay, I said it *appears* to be a simple fracture, but you'll need to have it X-rayed to be sure it's nothing more than that. A fall at your age…"

"I told you, it wasn't really a fall," Geneva

protested. "I tripped over a towel coming out of the bathroom and hit my arm against the sink. I never touched the floor."

"That doesn't matter," David cut in. "You're going to the hospital. Thank God we don't have to try to deal with this out in the middle of nowhere." He turned toward the doctor. "How far to the nearest hospital?"

"We can get her to her own doctor," Addy said. "I'll have Nick fly out here and pick her up."

"No!" Geneva exclaimed. "I can't leave now. I have a job to do. I promised Herbert…."

David ignored her. "Call him," he said to Addy. "Will he be able to take me, as well?"

"There should be just enough room." Without waiting for further discussion, Addy jumped up from her chair and headed for the door. "I'll set it up."

She went to the campground office to use the phone. Luckily Nick was still at the lodge. He promised to touch down at the campground in less than a hour.

When she returned to the cabin, she found Geneva sitting up in her bed, furious and weepy. Addy knew the woman was horribly disappointed about this turn of events, but there was no help for it. They simply couldn't take any chances with her health.

Addy began putting Geneva's belongings into her tote. "I don't know what you'll want or need," she told her as she scooped toiletries into the bag. "I'll just pack everything I can."

Geneva made a sniffing sound. "Suit yourself. No one seems to care what I think anyway."

David had left the cabin to settle up with the doctor. Addy didn't know how much time she and Geneva would have alone and she was desperate to take the old woman's mind off how miserable she was.

She came to sit beside her, offering a drink of water. "By the way," Addy said in an amused, knowing voice, "our waitress said thanks again for the extra tip. And that the next time you're back this way, she'll play Patsy Cline on the jukebox as many times as you want, absolutely free."

Color suddenly returned to Geneva's cheeks. "She was a very sweet young woman."

"Uh-huh," Addy said. "How many dollars' worth of quarters did she plug into that jukebox for you?"

"I don't know what you're talking about," the old woman replied and, in an obvious effort to avoid eye contact, reached down to smooth the blanket that covered her lower body.

"Pretend all you want, but David and I are wise to you."

Geneva's chin lifted. "Then you should at least have the decency to tell me what happened after I left the restaurant."

"Well…we got engaged."

"Oh, my heavens!"

"I'm joking. Sort of. Let David tell you all about it."

"Did he kiss you?"

"Yes. Twice."

"But that's wonderful! Just what I had hoped he would do."

A slight frown marred Addy's brow. "Geneva, don't read anything into it. We had fun tonight, but that's all it was."

"Of course it means something," Geneva said with the habitual tartness that disguised a very soft heart. "You know that."

Without even being aware of it, Addy readjusted the straps on Geneva's tote. "I'll bet David's kissed a lot of women in Hollywood."

"Dozens probably."

"Hundreds."

Geneva caught Addy's hand, drawing her attention so that their eyes met. "I know David has dated quite a lot of women out there. But in the last few years he seems to have actively avoided forming a serious relationship. He's like a little boy who finds out there's no Santa Claus so decides to call it quits on Christmas. But on this trip…well, maybe it's just an old woman's wishful thinking, but I've sensed a shift in him. As though something coiled very tight inside is relaxing."

"Really?" Addy posed with a grimace. "I haven't noticed much difference."

"And I'll tell you something else," Geneva went on. "He hasn't forgotten you, Addy. Or what you meant to him." Her mouth went taut as she motioned toward her injured arm. "If only this hadn't happened to spoil things."

David came back then, and there was no

more discussion on that subject, which pleased Addy because she honestly wasn't sure anymore what to think about David. If anything.

In no time at all Nick touched down on the campground's front lawn. Addy stood under the awning of the office with the owner, who had been a hovering presence since he'd found out about the accident. Probably trying to make sure no one was thinking lawsuit.

Bending low, she ran to meet Nick and shouted instructions over the *whoop-whoop* racket of the rotor's blades. Her brother had been a pilot in the Gulf war and didn't rattle easily. He'd already contacted Geneva's doctor and asked him to meet them at the hospital in Idaho Springs.

David came out of the cabin carrying his grandmother. She looked like a thwarted child. She buried her face against his sleeve, obviously hurt and angry.

"Geneva, please don't be this way," Addy said as she followed them to the helicopter. "It's for your own good."

The old woman gave her a flustered look.

"Oh, this is just terrible. Terrible. To be carted off to the hospital like a sack of potatoes. Leaving you here all by yourself. It's just not right. Not right at all."

"Someone has to stay with the animals." Addy tried to reason with her. "I'm going to regroup in the morning and head back to the lodge, so I'll see you very soon."

Geneva looked at her in disbelief. "I don't want you to make the trip back on your own. No! That won't do at all. Oh, I've made a mess of things. Such a mess…"

Nick leaned over his seat to catch Addy's eye. "You could fly them to the hospital, sis. I can bring the animals back for you."

Addy was tempted to accept. She certainly knew how to pilot the helicopter, and she wanted to be with Geneva. But she also knew that Nick was terrible with horses. Besides, there was a part of her that balked at having big brother take over. As though she couldn't finish this job on her own.

She shook her head at him. "Thanks, but let's leave it the way it is. I'll be fine."

Gently David laid his grandmother across the seat behind Nick, taking care not to jostle her left arm. Addy sent Geneva another smile and a kiss as David slid into the passenger seat.

"Don't let anything happen to her," she told him and she pressed Herbert's box into his hands.

He gave her an encouraging look. "I'll call the campground office as soon as I can and let you know what the doctor has to say. Try to get some rest." Addy nodded, and in the moment when she would have stepped away from the helicopter, David caught her up and pulled her close.

His mouth descended on hers, quick and hard and with authority. Then his lips moved against her ear. "This isn't the way I want to leave you, Addy. You know that, don't you?"

She blinked in surprise and stumbled away from the helicopter on legs that seemed made of wood with very few joints. It rose immediately, sending dust into a swirling dance and forcing her to close her eyes against the sting of sand. When she opened them, the craft was almost out of sight already.

In spite of the darkness, she thought she could still see David at the window, staring down at her, and in her mind she imagined that his face bore the lingering, hopeless look that accompanies a farewell.

CHAPTER TEN

SEATED IN THE WAITING room with Nick D'Angelo, David had to admit he was scared.

Halfway through the flight to the hospital Gran had suddenly begun to breathe heavier, and her skin had gone shiny with perspiration. With one quick look in David's direction, Nick had radioed that additional information to the hospital.

Had she had a heart attack? The new valve she'd gotten last year wouldn't do a bit of good if what was left of her old heart had decided not to cooperate.

David's stomach was doing acrobatics. He felt a helpless, futile rage rising within him and bore down on it resolutely.

Where was that damned doctor? What was taking him so long?

His eyes sought the double doors every time they spilled someone new into the room. The place was busy in spite of the late hour, but he hardly registered that there were others present.

Then the doctor came through the swinging doors. David and Nick rose and met him before he got halfway across the room.

"We're going to admit her," Dr. Nolan said without preamble. "The arm *is* broken, but it's a clean break. I'm more concerned about other things."

David nodded grimly. "Is it her heart?"

"Mr. McKay, your grandmother didn't have a heart attack. She had what we'd consider an *anxiety* attack. But just to be sure, I'd like to keep her for a few days and run tests."

David expelled a sigh of relief.

"However, I'm afraid there's a bit of a problem," Dr. Nolan went on. "Geneva is insisting on being discharged, and we can't keep her against her will. She doesn't even want to wait until the morning."

"She's not going anywhere," David said.

"Her anxiety level is still very high. We've done everything we can to calm her, but she's quite worked up about having left your guide alone at some campground."

"I'll talk to her."

Dr. Nolan smiled. "I was hoping you could reassure her. Geneva is one of my favorite patients, and I'd like to put her mind at ease."

It was morning by the time the medication his grandmother had been given wore off. David had been forced to get pretty stern with her about being discharged, but once the doctor had given her a sedative, that had put an end to it. He'd spent most of the hours before dawn seated beside her bed, listening to the rhythmic hiss and beep of hospital equipment.

Aware of movement from the bed, he turned his head to find Gran's clear blue gaze fixed on him. She seemed alert, and he thought the smile she gave him was one of the sweetest things he'd ever seen.

He flicked a quick glance toward her heart monitor.

"It's not my heart," she said in sulky displeasure. "I think I know enough now to tell when I'm fit as a May morning and when

I'm not." She made a restless movement. "I have to get out of here."

He pushed her gently back down. "Gran, take it easy—"

"I won't," she said with a mutinous shake of her head. "We've left things in a muddle back there and we've got to go back."

Again David's eyes cut to the monitor. His grandmother's heart rate was slightly higher now. Determinedly he leaned closer to the bed. His hand stroked her wrinkled cheek. "There's no reason to return."

David realized that for the first time in years she was angry with him. It was there in the flash of fire in her eyes. "There are two very good reasons to return. One, Herbert's ashes haven't been taken care of. I've failed him completely. And two, Addy is there."

"We can take care of Grampa's ashes some other time. Some other way. As for Addy, she'll be fine."

"She shouldn't be out there all by herself. And certainly not without you!"

"Haven't you been trying to convince me of what an efficient woman Addy is? If she has to make the trip back by herself—"

"You'd *let* her?" Gran's tone was incredulous.

His teeth clenched, and in a clutch for patience he rose and stalked to the window. He lifted one of the venetian blind slats and stared down vacantly into the parking lot. In his mind's eye he kept seeing Addy's figure getting smaller and smaller beneath the helicopter. There had been no choice, really. What else could he have done?

"Don't you care about her at all?" his grandmother asked.

He stood quietly for a moment. He wished he and Addy had had more time to talk. There was every possibility that the next time he saw her she would have found a way to put even more emotional distance between them—permanently.

He could envision how it would go. They'd mouth pleasant goodbyes. Then she'd go back to her life at the lodge. Maybe marry Brandon O'Dell. At the very least, she'd follow through on those plans for a baby.

As for him, when he was sure Gran was all right, he'd catch the next flight to L.A.

Immerse himself in meetings and e-mails. Dinner with acquaintances. Perhaps a private showing of some jackass movie. Anything— anything—not to be alone.

"David—"

He turned to face his grandmother. "Of course I care. But I have one of two choices. I can go back out there or I can stay here with you. I'm not leaving, Gran."

"But I told you—"

"May we come in?" a voice said from the door, and a second later Sam and Rose D'Angelo appeared.

Gran looked relieved and stretched out her fingers as though calling them closer. "Oh, Sam, I'm so glad to see you. Help me knock some sense into this ridiculous grandson of mine."

"It's all right. Calm down," Sam said, taking her hand.

Some silent subtext seemed to be going on between them. David frowned. He wondered what this was all about and realized that Rose D'Angelo's brow was knit in curiosity, too.

"Can Nick fly David back out to Addy?" Geneva asked. "With her help, he could take

Herbert's ashes to the Devil's Smile." She swung a glance toward David. "You'd do that for me, wouldn't you, dear? Please."

"Gran—"

"It would mean so much. I wanted to do it myself, but maybe that's part of the stress the doctor was talking about last night. Maybe I just can't bring myself to let him go." She sighed heavily. "But you could do it, David. I know you'd do it the right way. Please. For me."

"If I did, would you promise to stay here until the doctor has run every single test he wants to?"

"Yes. Absolutely."

"I suppose I could take care of it."

"Good," Geneva said, smiling. "And then you could help Addy get back? I don't like to think of her out there alone."

Rose D'Angelo spoke up. "Addy will be fine on her own. You mustn't worry."

Sam reached out to pat Geneva's hand. "Rose is right. Addy knows her stuff. She'll deal with any trouble that's foolish enough to show its face."

David frowned. "What kind of trouble?"

IN THE MORNING ADDY found a message tacked to her cabin door.

Gran okay. Stay where you are. I'll be in touch.

She was so relieved she nearly wept. The night had been lonely—filled with fear for Geneva. She'd always thought she had a knack for solitude, but Nick's helicopter had barely disappeared when she'd found herself longing for company. And news. Not knowing had been unbearable.

She knew she could make the trip home by herself. It would be tricky with the mules, keeping them in line, but she could manage it. If she pushed hard, she could be back at Lightning River Lodge in half the time it had taken to get out here.

She couldn't wait to see Geneva again. See for herself that the woman was really all right. And she must be or David would have told her, wouldn't he?

Geneva was lucky to have him in her life. In spite of his unwillingness to come home very often, he really did love her.

An unexpected prickling behind her eyes

made her lose patience with herself. Just relief making her feel sentimental.

Clementine's wasn't open for breakfast, so Addy settled for coffee from the campground store and took it out to the picnic tables, where a sweet morning breeze teased the air. Soon she'd start packing up all the extra supplies she'd brought. Since it was just going to be her on the return trip, she could keep to the bare minimum. Getting home—that's all that mattered.

And when she got home, would David still be there?

If Geneva was all right, would he have gone back to Los Angeles already?

Addy hugged her knees up to her chest, then laid her head across her arms. Her thoughts drifted.

Never seeing David again. Wasn't that what she wanted? For him to be gone, out of her life as quickly as possible?

She heard the *whoop-whoop* of a helicopter and lifted her head. Nick's R44 Raven was setting down on the campground lawn again. She was surprised to see him and even more surprised when David stepped out of the passenger side. He ducked down and, when he was well away from the craft, waved Nick away. The chopper lifted off almost as quickly as it had landed.

Chewing on her lip, Addy watched David approach. He looked fresh and clean but tired. And he was smiling.

When he reached her, he said, "Turns out, I missed your coffee." He set his duffel bag on the ground.

"Is Geneva really all right?" she asked faintly.

He nodded. "The doctor is taking good care of her. She should be in the hospital a few days for observation."

"Why aren't you with her?"

"Because in order to get her to agree to stay there, I had to swear I'd take care of Grampa's ashes, then see you safely back to the lodge."

"I can manage just fine by myself."

"That's what everyone seems to think. Gran, however, was adamant. Especially after your father mentioned the possibility of hungry mountain lions and rogue bears."

"Bears and mountain lions?" Addy said

with a frown. "There's never been an attack in this area that I'm aware of."

"That's what Nick told me on the way out here. But it's too late now. I'm here. Back in the saddle, it seems."

"I'm sorry. I know this is the last place you want to be."

David made a face. "Don't be so sure. I'm sort of getting the hang of this camping thing. And I'd like to finish what Gran started." He slapped his hands together, rubbing them back and forth. "Now where do we go from here, trail boss?"

THEY TRIMMED DOWN supplies and stabled Gran's horse at the campground for pickup on the way back home. By late afternoon, pushing hard, they reached the Devil's Smile.

To David, it seemed almost anticlimactic at first. When they entered the canyon, it appeared to be just another secluded gorge of sandstone cliffs and stunted pines.

But as they led the horses along the winding river that cut through the ravine, the sun began to slide down the sides of the canyon walls, favoring them with a spectacular light show. The cliffs blazed with color—every shade of red, orange and gold. Even pink and purple. And while other canyons could boast the same variety of mineral deposits in the rock, there was one difference that set the Devil's Smile apart: the effect erosion had had in shaping the stone.

The canyon was a natural amphitheater of sculpted rock formations, a wonderful jumbled collection of spires, stalactites and sentinels. An imaginative mind could see fanciful figures in the stone—soldiers, melting castles, turbaned women in flowing robes. It didn't disappoint, and David suddenly understood why his grandparents had been so charmed by the place.

They pulled their horses to a halt, by some unspoken agreement preferring to set up camp in the dark rather than give up one moment of the magic show that sundown was creating.

"It's so beautiful…." Addy said on a note of awe.

"It is. Just the way Gran described it. No wonder Grampa Herb loved it so much." He dismounted, then dug around in one of the packs on Bounder's back. "I have to get some of this on film for Gran."

After dark, they made camp near the river. Dinner was an oddly silent affair. David noticed that, for the first time, Addy seemed to have no appetite and only picked at her food.

Later she wandered off. He gave her a few minutes, then set out, as well. The animals were tethered a hundred yards away in a natural corral of red rock and young trees. Addy wasn't with them.

He headed toward the river. The current was fast and rippled noisily over the rocks, so that confetti flecks of moonlight sparkled on its surface. He spotted Addy off to his right, lying on a huge boulder.

Since leaving the campground, he and Addy had been pleasant to one another but nothing more than that. Once they were back in the saddle, they seemed to have lost a little ground. He wasn't certain how he should feel about that. Part of him said it was for the best. Another part argued for more.

Damn it! She could pretend all she wanted,

but she *had* responded to that kiss on the cabin porch. He hadn't misread or imagined that.

He approached her quietly. She was flat on her back, a pair of binoculars pointed skyward. Pebbles crunched beneath David's hiking shoes, and she sat up suddenly and turned.

"What's up there tonight?" he asked.

"I've just found the Leo constellation." She offered him the binoculars and slid to one side of the boulder.

Sometimes fate just decided to lend a hand, he thought as he sat beside her. Maybe it was perverse determination that kept her on the rock—the compulsion not to appear intimidated—but he was pleased when she didn't move away.

"What am I looking for?" he asked, raising the binoculars.

"Lie flat. Otherwise you don't get the size and magnitude."

He did as she instructed. The rocky perch felt cool and hard against his back. "All right. Now what?" he asked, fiddling with the focus until the images sharpened.

Patiently Addy explained how to get his bearings in what she called the "sky vault."

Old high school lessons came back, and he began to pick out some of the simpler constellations.

After about ten minutes he lowered the binoculars and levered up on his elbows. He lay silent, hearing his own heartbeats like thunder because Addy was wonderfully close.

He wondered if she could sense his desire. Her face was lifted to the sky as she pointed out some star. Under his consuming gaze, she turned her head to look at him as people often do when they're being watched.

He thought how amazingly beautiful she was, lying there in the moonlight. The desperate longing to hold her spread, leaving him feeling reckless.

"They never seem this bright at home," he said.

"Too many ground lights," Addy explained.

More silence stretched between them. To soften it, he lifted the binoculars again. "My astronomy's pretty rusty," he said. "Only one semester in high school, and I'm afraid all the guys wanted to get to Sex Ed. Better pictures."

Her lips tickled into a smile. The sight of

it made him want to catch her mouth in a kiss. And wonder, too, just how much longer he could hold out or even why he should. A slight shift of his hips, and she could be in his arms. *If* she was willing.

He swallowed hard and scanned the velvet darkness for a way to keep his libido leashed. "Where's Arcturus? I remember that one. We used to get a kick out of finding Virgo." He wiggled his eyebrows wickedly at her. "The *virgin*."

"The maiden, actually. Look at the end of Leo's tail and take a left."

"Oh, yeah. There she is. And what about Andromeda?"

"Wrong time of the year for Andromeda."

"Too bad. I always liked that story about the beautiful princess chained to the rock."

She plucked the binoculars out of his grasp. "Probably because of the babe-bondage element."

He gave her a wounded look. "Actually I liked the part about Perseus slaying the sea monster to save her."

She frowned, but her face was losing its armor.

They sat in wordless intimacy for a time, marooned in a silvery disk of moonlight. The breeze combed through the pines and whispered over their skin like the touch of silk.

Addy sighed. "Back at the lodge, I'll sometimes take the guests out so we can stargaze. On a clear night, there's nothing like it. Absorbing the peace and quiet, watching for shooting stars. Guess that seems pretty tame to you."

"Tame. But not undesirable."

She gave him a look of idle speculation. "Why don't you come back to Broken Yoke more often, David? Do you really hate it so much?"

"I don't hate it."

"Then…is it because of me?"

He met her eyes. "I haven't forgotten what we said to one another that last night. How ugly it got. I just thought it would be easier on both of us if I stayed away."

"I'm sorry you felt that way. I wouldn't—"

"Don't apologize. Right now it feels as though I wasted a lot of years keeping my distance. I've missed you, Addy."

He turned toward her then, because there

was nothing else he could do, really. His stomach was in a knot only kissing her could untie.

One breeze-ruffled curl had fallen against her cheek. He captured it between two fingers, then used it to trace the line of her jaw. She made no move to stop him and, in fact, lay quite still, staring up at him with an odd look of expectation.

Bending, he let his lips brush hers. He kept the contact brief and light, giving her time to adjust. Her hands arrived at his chest, and he lifted them over her head to pin them gently against the stone.

"You look like Andromeda lying here like this," he whispered. His teeth nibbled at the softness of her earlobe. "Poor little captive. Do you need rescuing?"

"No," she replied, but she took a shaky breath. "And if I did need rescuing, I'm not sure if it'd be *by* you or *from* you."

He laughed lightly. "*By* me, my suspicious princess. Let me show you how Perseus made Andromeda purr with pleasure."

She gave him the skeptical glance of a cynic who had long ago given up on fantasy.

When he moved to take her lips again, she pulled one of her hands out of his light hold and brought it back between them. "I don't need rescuing. I'm a very self-sufficient woman."

"Very self-sufficient. And very much a woman."

He slid the top button of her blouse from its home. She pushed his hand away. "Can't we just talk?"

"Talk then," he encouraged. "I can do more than one thing at a time." She made an agitated move to rise, and he stopped her. There was an edge of panic in her eyes, as though her very survival was an issue here. Finding a control he thought he'd lost, he gave her a slow, reassuring smile. "All right. What do you want to talk about?"

She wet her lips. "Why haven't you ever married?"

He ignored her female tactics to kill the mood. He played with the top button on her blouse. "I've never found anyone I could imagine spending the rest of my life with."

"In a place as full of beautiful women as Hollywood?"

He nodded absently. "Especially not there. It's not a town where relationships thrive."

"Maybe it's you."

"Me?"

"It's easy to say Hollywood is to blame, but maybe you're just a love-'em-and-leave-'em kind of guy. You certainly ditched me fast enough ten years ago."

He scowled. The moment was fading. With the back of his hand he stroked the wisps of hair at her temple, then let his finger wander over one delicate ear. "Do you really want to waste this beautiful evening talking about the past?"

He separated the edges of her collar, exposing her throat to the moonlight. Gently he let his hand slide down until he found her pulse. Her lashes drifted shut.

"Your past shapes the person you are today," she said on a mere whisper of sound.

"Assuming that one learns the lesson it offers."

Her eyes opened to regard him with dark interrogation. "And did you?"

"Only too well."

"Then it shouldn't make you uncomfortable to talk about it."

His hand slipped beneath the material of her blouse to brush across one of her breasts. It seemed as cool and smooth as satin, and she squirmed slightly under his touch. "It doesn't," he said. "I just think there are more interesting things to discuss. Like us, for instance."

"There is no 'us.'"

"Sure there is. You, me—us. It's a pretty simple concept, D'Angelo."

"Not to me it isn't," she said in a stumbling rush.

He saw enough pleasure in her face to impel him to seek her nipple, caressing it to erection. "Well, that's because you like to mess it up with a lot of overthinking. Has it occurred to you that we're two adults? That we're still attracted to one another after all these years?" His hand cupped her breast. "What's wrong with exploring where that can lead?"

She quivered. "I know where it can lead." She gasped and arched upward as his hand tightened infinitesimally on her flesh. "No place either of us should go."

Her voice had hitched and gone small, and

he knew he was taking unfair advantage now. He should let her go. He should let her up. But how could he when the old abiding ache he hadn't felt in so long had hold of him once again? And Addy was with him in this. Her resistance was crumbling like wet sugar.

"I'm not trying to make you lose control of your life, Addy. I only want you to lose control of your breathing." He lowered his head, nuzzling the top of her breast.

Her hands took his hair in an effort to force his head back. "I don't want this."

"Really? Why would you deny yourself the pleasure? Don't say you don't like it—not with your heart beating the way it is against my mouth." His tongue teased another response and he said softly against her flesh, "This, Addy? Is this what you don't want? Your body doesn't seem to be listening."

Her head whipped back and forth. "Don't…"

"Too late, I think…"

"Stop…"

"You can stop me in a minute," he whispered thickly. "Right now, kiss me."

He didn't wait for her to respond. Instead he kissed her with a kind of triumph. If she really wanted him to stop, she was sending all the wrong signals. She'd given up fighting him, fighting herself—at least for now.

Suddenly she was kissing him back, quick to ferret out his secrets, so that his excitement grew and her touch left him feeling suffocated.

But he should have known the miracle couldn't hold. Addy's body jerked. She tore her mouth away. Her breath came in long, shaky waves, and a look of glassy horror lay in her eyes because, he sensed, her response had been only half against her will.

But already he could feel her mentally drawing away from him, clawing her way back second by second. He hated to see the changes—the hardening around her mouth, the vertical line between her eyes.

He brushed her warm, soft lips with a fingertip, determined not to easily relinquish this golden moment. "You know, princess, if you keep kissing me like that, I'm the one who'll need rescuing."

Her dark eyes met his, but they had lost some of their sparkle. Stiffly she rebuttoned her blouse. "Let me up," she demanded, her voice as hard and cold as a jewel.

His starved heart made him reluctant to comply. "Is there any good reason why I should?"

"Because in a week you'll be back in Los Angeles and all this will be just an obligation you've fulfilled. I don't intend to provide you with cocktail-party gossip or be the butt of a few jokes you share in the steam room of your club."

This unexpected piece of brutality left him more surprised than if she had doused him with freezing water. The strong, electrifying attraction was slain. Years ago, out by the lake, she'd accused him of some pretty serious offenses. But did she still see him that way?

After a dangerous pause, he pulled away. She sat up, intent on scrambling down from the boulder. Before she could make her escape, he caught her wrist in a hard grasp and swung her back to face him. "I don't blame you for being confused, Addy. Frankly I'm a little surprised by all this myself. But I'm not the testosterone-driven mongrel you once accused me of being."

It seemed to him that every trace of color had left her face. He might have just captured a ghost in the moonlight. "I'm sorry if you think I'm being unfair," she said. "I just know that when I'm not paying attention, you slip past my defenses and go to my head like wine. You're much too potent for someone like me, David. You always were."

"Forget about the way things *were*."

"I can't. I loved you. And you hurt me." She looked away. "And now you can hurt me again if I let you. I'm on the verge of making one of the biggest decisions of my life. I don't need distractions right now. Especially when they won't mean a damned thing to someone like you."

"Someone like me? That's exactly what you wanted once upon a time."

"I know that. But that was a long time ago. And knowing what you wanted out of life, knowing how eager you were to get out of Broken Yoke, I should never have let it go so far."

He lifted his free hand to her lean, high cheekbone. It could have been carved from marble. "I wanted you to come with me to

Los Angeles. If you loved me, why didn't you even consider it?"

"Because I was scared to death. Scared to give up my family, everything I loved about living in Broken Yoke, of trying to make a new home in a strange place with a man who didn't believe in commitment. I couldn't imagine how we could make it."

"We would have managed."

She shook her head with a glazed and cautious look of someone who fears that the first blink will cause tears to run down her face. "Maybe we would have. But I wasn't willing to chance it. Not with a baby on the way."

CHAPTER ELEVEN

HIS EYES RESTED ON her face with a kind of incredulity that she could see even in the pale moonlight. A lock of hair had tumbled across his forehead, but it could not soften the shock in his features.

"A baby?" he said at last, as though trying on the word. "You were pregnant? How? When?"

"Well, I think we know how," she said nervously. "And the *when* part of it...I'm guessing the night of the Halloween dance. Up on Wildcat Ridge. You remember that night?"

"Vividly. But why didn't you tell me?"

She gave him a sharp, challenging look and then squeezed her eyes shut. This wasn't the way she had envisioned telling him. If ever. She opened her eyes. "When would I have slipped that news in?" she asked him.

"Before or after we finished calling each other every name in the book?"

His eyebrows descended in a frown. "Okay. Admittedly that wasn't the right time. But why not later? Once we were past the heat of the moment, why didn't you call me?"

"When? The next day you left for Hollywood with the rest of the film crew. You had big plans. How was the prospect of being a father supposed to compete with all that? Especially when there had never been any question about how you felt about kids."

He ran a distracted hand through his hair. "For God's sake, Addy, surely you had to know—"

"I didn't know anything," she cut in quickly. Then just as suddenly her anger faded. "In the end, it didn't matter anyway."

Another silence. There seemed to be an awful lot of them. When she didn't continue right away, David said at last, "You lost the baby."

She could barely nod. "A few days later I miscarried. Leslie told me it just happens that way sometimes. But it felt like the end of everything. I wanted to call you, but then it seemed so pointless. It just seemed more sensible to move on, to put the past behind me. I never told Mom or Dad. Only Leslie. She's a nurse and she knew what I should do."

He pulled her into his arms. She wanted to sink deeper into his embrace, because there was some ridiculous incurable hope inside her that something could be salvaged from all this.

"I'm sorry you went through that alone," he said against her ear. "I wish you had told me. I had a right to know."

She pulled away, searching for his eyes in the moonlight. "Well, you know now. And what I'd really like is not to talk about it anymore. What I'd really like is for you to let me go."

THE NEXT MORNING ADDY went through her trail routine under a weight of depression too crushing even for tears.

David had unnerved her last night. A more clever woman would have played the game the way it was meant to be played, taken the heady pleasure of his kisses, perhaps even found a way to turn his interest to her advantage.

But then, a more clever woman would never have allowed herself to fall in love with a man who had once broken her heart.

The whole truth came rolling up toward her like a breaker on the sand. She was still in love with David McKay, and wretchedly so, just as she had feared from the moment she saw him at Geneva's.

When David emerged from the tent, he was pleasant but distant. Wrapped in her own dark thoughts, Addy found that she could not hold her eyes to his long enough to find out his true state of mind. She tried her best to keep the conversation as natural and intelligent as possible, which wasn't saying much.

Finally, unable to stand the silence, she jumped up and threw the dregs of her coffee into the fire. A pervading sense of loss threatened to submerge her as she turned to him. "I'm going to check on the animals. I assume you'll want to take care of your grandmother's wishes as soon as possible."

"I'm going to take care of it this morning."

Her throat too tight for speech, she could only nod sharply. Then she hastened down the trail to where she'd hobbled the horses last night.

The coffee had soured in her stomach, and her eyes burned, but she refused to give in to sorrow. The fact that she was still in love with David didn't change a thing.

He might have wound his way back into her heart, but she knew he had every intention of winding himself right back out. Hollywood, with all its glamour and excitement and business successes, awaited his return. He might flirt and caress and lust after her, but all the glorious sunsets, velvet nights and foolishly acquiescent women in the world wouldn't keep him from catching the first plane out when this trip was over.

As for her…well, she still wanted a baby more than anything in the world, and a sperm bank seemed the sensible answer. She couldn't imagine agreeing to marry Brandon now. She just didn't love him, and no matter how much easier it might make it for her to raise a child, it wouldn't be fair to him. He deserved more than gratitude from a woman.

She could get a handle on her lacerated emotions. She could. The strange adaptability of the human fabric would begin to operate within her, just as it had ten years ago. She couldn't keep David in her life. But she could make darned sure she continued to have one of her own worth living.

She had this trip to complete. And probably more after this one. She had obligations. The family depended on her. And more than anything else, she had a baby to plan for.

Feeling a little better, she gave all the animals a good rubdown. Physical work would help put things in perspective. She didn't need to waste any more time or energy wishing things could be different or lamenting that they weren't.

DAVID WALKED OUT INTO the canyon, the box containing his grandfather's ashes tucked under one arm. He had no idea where the right spot was, but Gran had tried to describe it for him, hoping that he might find where they had camped on their honeymoon.

There were lots of pretty places along

the river, ideal for campsites. But nothing seemed…right. He followed the water for a few more minutes, then eventually came to a spot where it widened and gurgled around a spill of huge boulders. On either side large cottonwoods created a sheltered haven. From Gran's description, this had to be it.

He worked his way across the stones to stand on one of the large boulders that angled out over the water. He could imagine his grandparents dangling their legs in the water, laughing over how good its coolness felt against their tired feet. He couldn't picture them young and nimble, but they'd always had a zest for life that he'd admired.

He looked down at the box in his hands. It was crudely carved, not at all what he'd have expected Gran to pick for her husband's ashes, but she'd never been given to fancy knickknacks anyway.

"Here we are, Grampa," David said, clearing his throat. "Your favorite spot. Just as Gran promised."

His heart raced. Since it was still early in the morning, the sun was just peeking over the rim of the high canyon walls, touching all the shaded crevices of rock with light. It was pink and gold and so bright; it spangled on the water.

The lid of the box slipped off easily once he managed the latches. With his gaze fixed on the canyon walls, David held out his hands and tilted the container.

"Goodbye, Grampa," David said softly. "Gran misses you and will always love you. Me, too. More than I ever took the time to say."

The breeze took over. The ashes swirled in an updraft of air, drifting over the water a few moments before settling in the current. Some of the particles carried farther, dancing on sunbeams to descend finally on the opposite bank and become one with the earth, sifting over the plants like pollen.

The little ceremony over, he dropped down on the boulder and sat quietly for a long time. He started to replace the lid on the box, then noticed that there was an inscription under the top.

For Gennie, it read. With Undying Love. Your Herbert.

David smiled, thinking of the time and love that had gone into the making of this box. Had any two people been more in love? He'd been so lucky to have them.

The years he'd spent with his grandparents had been wonderful. In some ways, better than the years he'd had with his parents.

His father had always had the same wanderlust and thirst for adventure as *his* own parents had, and though David had loved his mom and dad, they had often left him in the hands of well-paid nannies. Addy thought he hated kids, but he didn't. The truth was, every time he found himself handed off to someone else while his parents went on their way without him, David had made a promise to himself never to be that kind of parent. If you couldn't spend time with them, what was the point in even having kids?

The thought of children made David think of Addy. How hard it must have been to go through losing their baby without anyone but a family friend to help her get through it. She should have called him, damn it. She should have called.

But getting Addy to do anything she didn't want to was one tough task. She was stubborn like her old man and headstrong.

When had David ever been able to tell her what to do? It had been one of the things he had loved most about her. That unwillingness to take any crap from him.

Was she really going to go through with this sperm-bank idea? Or marry Brandon O'Dell, who would be kind and thoughtful and always ready with a baby bottle but was probably boring as hell? How could Addy give up on finding real love?

David glanced skyward. The clouds were like cotton, the blue so piercing against his eyes that he had to squint.

"She needs someone to love her the way you loved Gran," he said aloud to the breeze. "Got any ideas, Grampa?"

But the air became still and silent.

"Everything all right?"

Addy looked up from Sheba's front hoof to find David approaching. She dropped the horse's leg and dusted her hands together.

"Just doing a little maintenance," she told him. "How about you?" she asked, motioning toward the box tucked under his arm. "How did it go?"

"Fine. I think Gran will be very pleased."

"Good. We should be able to leave in a few minutes if you'd like. I know we're both eager to get back."

He cocked his head at her. "Are we? I've been thinking about last night…."

Addy made a restive movement. "We don't need to talk about last night."

He hooked the fingers of one hand into the back of his jeans. "Maybe you don't need to, but I do. I've been giving it some thought. Maybe there's a way we could start fresh—"

His words startled her, but she lifted her chin, determined not to let any false hopes build. "David, don't."

"Why? I want to see you again. California's not that far away. We could visit back and forth. Make time for one another."

"It's impossible."

"I'll ask you again—why? Because you intend to marry O'Dell? I don't believe that will ever happen."

"Maybe it will and maybe it won't. But what *will* happen is that I'm going to have a baby to take care of very soon. I certainly won't have time for trips to and from Holly-wood."

"I see women with babies on planes all the time. I'm not saying it's fun, but it certainly seems manageable."

"That's not the way *I* want to raise a child."

He shook his head impatiently. "It could work, Addy."

"No, it couldn't."

He looked frustrated, but in the moment before he could say any more, she left him standing there and headed back to camp.

She couldn't imagine what had gotten into him. How could he propose such an idea? Start fresh? How could they? And what possible point could there be in it?

ADDY SET A BRISK PACE, and by that afternoon they had returned to the campground where Geneva had broken her arm. They called the hospital to discover that David's grand-mother was keeping her promise and allowing the doctors to run all the tests they wanted. They picked up Clover from the stable, replenished a few supplies and headed out again.

There had been little conversation between them. At least nothing too personal. Addy was determined to keep it that way.

By sundown they were past the halfway point. Riding side by side, they moved along a steep, treeless ridge. Fifty feet down on her right lay a dry riverbed.

Up here on the rim, the ground was soft and crumbly beneath the horses' hooves, and they kicked up more dust than usual. *We'll need to heat lots of water tonight,* Addy thought. They'd look like desert rats by the time they got off this ridge.

Bounder's lead rope, tied to her saddle, suddenly went taut. Miserable mule! *I'm not in the mood for your games. Keep going ornery on me and I'll sell you for dog food yet.*

"Knock it off, Bounder!" she snapped, turning to grab handfuls of the leather line so she could jerk him into cooperation.

She saw then that the mule had stubbornly decided to stop to shoo a pestering deerfly away from his haunches. The animal pounded his hind legs into the ground and slapped his tail back and forth. But in the next moment the fly landed on Bounder's rump and bit deeply. The mule bawled furiously and jumped forward, colliding with Sheba.

Everything happened quickly after that.

It didn't matter that Sheba and Bounder had been stablemates for years—the mare didn't like having the mule practically on top of her. She kicked out, then began to sidle out of the way.

"Easy, girl," Addy coaxed, shortening her grip on the reins. There was no fear in her. She knew every move the mare was likely to make.

David had pulled his horse to a halt. His head swung to give her a concerned look. "You all right...?"

"We're fine," she reassured him quickly over the noise of Bounder's outraged braying. "Just a little disagreement over personal space."

But in that moment Sheba's back hooves slid off the level trail. The loose sand shifted, unbalancing the animal, and to compensate, Addy threw herself forward onto her neck.

Unfortunately Bounder was still tethered to them. As the distance between the two animals widened, the mule jerked back in fright. The lead line tangled in Sheba's hind legs and she stumbled. The leather snapped, and both horse and rider slid farther down the slope, starting a minor rock slide.

Desperate to get Sheba's head up, Addy yanked hard on the reins, but she knew it was too late. It was impossible to keep the horse from falling. She heard David's harsh shout from the trail. Sheba's stumbling plunge threatened to send the animal down to her knees, and before that happened, Addy knew she had to get out of the saddle. She kicked out of the stirrups and jumped.

The soft sand cushioned Addy's fall, but it was still hard enough to knock the wind out of her. Momentum sent her cartwheeling further. Rocks skittered down the incline with her, bruising her skin, and weeds tore and plucked at her clothes. She came to an ungraceful, painful halt halfway down the slope. Her head struck something with enough force that spots danced in front of her eyes.

Out of breath and barely conscious, she lay there listening to the sound of pebbles bouncing the rest of the way to the riverbed, someone shouting in the distance and Sheba's frightened whinny.

Sheba. Please don't let her be hurt.

And then everything went very bright yellow in front of her eyes and all the noises collided into one high whine as she blacked out.

CHAPTER TWELVE

SHE COULDN'T HAVE BEEN unconscious very long, because she was still on the rocky slope when next she opened her eyes. Someone had spoken her name. Squinting up into the bright sunlight, she realized that David was kneeling over her. She frowned and tried to rise.

His hand pushed her firmly back down. "Lie still," he told her gruffly, and Addy was certain that the words hadn't come out as steady and detached as he might have wished.

She swallowed. Her mouth was unbearably dry and felt coated with dust. "That mule's in trouble now. I told him I was going to sell him for dog food."

Gently his fingers pulled clinging strands of hair away from her face. His hands began a light, hurried exploration of her arms and legs. "Does anything feel broken?"

Her head hurt. Really hurt. "The more logical question would be, does anything *not* feel broken? Is Sheba all right?" she asked, trying to catch sight of the animal.

"She's up. Not injured that I can see. We can worry about her later. Right now I want to get you up this hill." He glanced up the slope, then back at her. "I know there are all kinds of rules about moving an injured person, but I can't see that it's good for you to lie here any longer. Can you put your arms around my neck?"

"You can't carry me up this hill."

"Thanks for the vote of confidence."

"I can walk," she protested.

"Be quiet and don't argue."

Carefully David lifted her in his arms. She couldn't help the groan of pain that slid past her lips. He climbed through the thick dirt slowly, and she could tell he was trying to absorb every jostling step. Foolish tears welled in her eyes at his consideration, and she turned her nose into his chest. The warm fragrance of his skin reached her through his shirt. Even her jumbled senses couldn't fail to register that pleasure.

"Hang on," he said as though sensing her sudden distress. "Only a little farther."

She blinked hard, realizing that the stain across the front of his shirt was blood. "You're bleeding."

"Not me, little idiot. You."

"Oh." She tilted her head back and found him silently regarding her. His mouth was drawn in a tight line of exasperation, but concern darkened the blue of his eyes. "Don't worry," she reassured him. "Head wounds bleed a lot."

"It's not your head. You've just got a bump there. Looks like you have a couple of deep scratches but nothing that needs stitching. You have a first-aid kit?"

She nodded, which was probably a mistake, because it set off a renewed clanging in her head.

"Damn!" His voice was a mixture of anger and frustration. "I wish we'd brought liquor on this trip."

"I don't want to get drunk on top of everything else."

"Not for you. For me. You took ten years off my life when I saw you go flying."

"Once I catch my breath, I'll be…all right." The cold nauseated feeling was starting to spread. She clamped her lips together and squeezed her eyes shut, determined not to embarrass herself any further.

"If you feel like you're going to pass out again, don't hold back on my account."

"I didn't faint," she managed to say sharply. "I never faint. I'm not the fainting type."

And then, because the Fates always took perverse enjoyment in showing her how wrong she could be, she fainted dead away.

As a kid, David had once been bitten by a snake.

He had been visiting his grandparents, playing in their backyard, and found an old mason jar just perfect for saving pennies. Unfortunately, when he'd picked it up, he'd discovered that a small snake had decided to claim the jar, as well. Before David had realized it, the startled reptile had bit him on the hand.

All the way to the hospital emergency

room, with Grampa Herb driving too fast and Gran telling him to slow down, David had believed he was going to die. His hand had been only slightly swollen, the blood almost nonexistent, but he had known that he was done for. All the bad guys in the Saturday-matinee Westerns died when a snake bit them. In screaming, bloated agony.

He hadn't screamed. He hadn't cried. But what he had experienced was a mind-numbing coldness that radiated from the pit of his stomach to all his extremities. Oddly enough, in spite of the ice in his veins, he'd been sweating. And his heart—he'd been absolutely certain that it was free-floating in his chest, a quivering mass that had suddenly decided it could no longer perform.

Of course, he hadn't died. The villain had been a harmless garter snake, not a rattler or sidewinder. If anything, the snakebite had given him a certain badge of honor with his buddies when he got back home. In his limited world, no one had ever been bitten before and lived to tell about it.

But since that day he had never forgotten just how scared you could get. Throat-drying, speech-robbing fear could twist your insides like someone practicing sailor's knots with your intestines. And he had never stopped being grateful that in all the intervening years he had never come close to being that afraid ever again.

Until today.

Until Sheba had backed off the side of that steep incline and taken Addy along.

He barely remembered sliding off Injun Joe. Then he had plunged over the side, his boots sinking deep in the sand. A few feet away Sheba, reins trailing in the dirt, had been waiting nervously, but all David could see was the blue of Addy's jeans and the lighter blue of her blouse, lying awkwardly and still against a good-size rock.

His soul had contracted in one sick sense of coming doom. Somehow he got down the slope, though how he didn't know, with his legs gone at the knees and the sure knowledge that the sight of death, swift and unkind, was the only thing waiting for him.

That old snakebitten feeling had its fangs in him then. He had felt it coiling around his heart, squeezing the life out of him.

He'd wanted to howl.

He'd wanted to hit something.

Finding Addy alive had allowed him to save himself from the brink of an abyss and left him light-headed, shaking with relief. The strength and significance of his reaction was not lost on him, but at that crucial moment it was a thought to file away until the crisis had passed.

Somehow by the time Addy had opened her eyes and stared hazily up at him he had mastered his emotions. Fear had begun to lose its grip.

Now, sitting cross-legged beside Addy in the tent, he waited for her to wake up. Movement caught his eye, and he turned his head to find her shifting in her sleep. He stroked a silky curl away from her forehead, using the opportunity to check for a fever. There was none.

He had slipped her into the oversized T-shirt she'd slept in and left her in her panties from the waist down. One of her bare legs had emerged from under the sleeping bag. Other than the darkening bruise on one knee, that leg was just about as perfect as God could create—elegantly long, creamy perfection. He lifted her hand in his, inspecting the scrapes along her palm. The soft skin was red and would no doubt be sore and stiff tomorrow, but he'd removed the embedded dirt. With the exception of that nasty bump on the back of her head, he didn't believe any of Addy's injuries were worse than this.

He brought her hand to his mouth, letting his lips lie against the warm cup of her palm for a long time. Touching her was a mistake. If he knew what was good for him, he would cudgel his senses back into cool discipline.

Her fingers stirred against his cheek and he released them slowly. Turning his head, he saw that her gaze was on him, in that scowling concentration of a person who suspects gaps of time may be missing from their memory.

"I didn't faint," she said clearly.

"Okay," he replied with a slight smile. "You didn't."

"I was sleeping."

"You needed it. Still got a twenty-one-gun salute going off in your head?"

"Not too bad. How's Sheba?"

"A lot better off than you."

She looked relieved. "I'll survive. Give me a few minutes to change clothes—"

She levered herself upward, trying to get her elbows under her.

"Whoa," he said, placing a hand against her shoulder. "You're not going anywhere. We're staying put for the night. We'll see how you feel in the morning."

"But—"

"You've got a bump on your head the size of a hen's egg. I've already set up camp. Did a pretty good job of it, if I do say so myself. So now you're going to be a good girl and get as much rest as possible."

She was staring at him, annoyed and obviously frustrated. "I thought we were clear on this. I'm in charge out here."

He shook his head and said in a smoothly emphatic voice, "Sorry, trail boss, there's been a mutiny. Live with it."

Her mouth tightened. "You're a...a bully."

"Now I know you're brain damaged if that's the best insult you can manage." He poured a cup of water from a canteen and held it out to her. She took it eagerly. His other hand came behind her head. "Lift up. I want you to swallow these."

In his open palm lay two pills. She frowned down at them. "What is it?"

"You don't recognize aspirin?"

He watched her closely while she took the pills from his palm with a resigned sigh and washed them down.

"You know, you have absolutely no bedside manner," she complained as she settled back on the makeshift bedding.

"It's the Hollywood influence. No one expects you to be likable there."

"So that explains your success."

His lips twitched and he ran the back of his fingers gently along her cheek. "Wound me, Addy. It only reassures me that no real harm was done."

"David, this is silly…."

"If you feel all right tomorrow, I promise you can go back to running things. But for tonight your body is in my hands."

"I'm not sure I like the sound of that."

He laughed.

In spite of his objections, Addy insisted

that she be allowed up long enough to see for herself that, except for a small scrape along her withers, which David had already seen to, Sheba was unhurt. He stayed close by her side, ready to steady her if she stumbled or swayed. But when she had finished, and he pushed aside the tent flap so she could lie down once more, she balked.

"I want to stay outside," she said. "Tonight I really would like to see the stars."

In the end, he brought her sleeping bag out of the tent and placed it near the campfire.

For dinner he fixed her two bowls of soup. She put up only token resistance at having her request for some of the leftover spaghetti refused.

"Too heavy on a nervous stomach," he vetoed.

"I don't have a nervous stomach."

"And you're not going to get one."

"I should take care of the animals."

"I've done it. Even gave them rubdowns while you were sleeping. How's the headache?"

"Gone."

"You never were a very good liar."

Addy frowned at him. "I don't need babysitting."

"Good," he remarked with a shrug. He shook more aspirin into her palm. "Swallow these and we'll both get some sleep."

She was evidently too tired to fight it. He could tell from the way she moved that her body was stiffening more with every passing hour.

He sat cross-legged beside her. "Turn over. Before you go to sleep I'm going to give you a back rub. Maybe you won't be quite so sore in the morning."

She opened her mouth to protest, then seemed to think better of it. Pillowing her head on her arms, Addy shifted onto her stomach and watched the flames of the campfire flicker in a mesmerizing dance as he gently kneaded the calves of her legs. He felt every tightened nerve ending begin to unwind.

"Now doesn't that feel good?" he asked.

"No. It feels *wonderful*."

His hands moved to her back now, and Addy didn't argue. She nudged the baggy T-shirt up out of the way while he massaged lotion onto either side of her spine in slow ever-widening circles.

She groaned a sound of pure pleasure. "I could kiss you for this. And I promise, tomorrow night I'll give *you* the back rub."

"I'll hold you to that."

"David?" she began hesitantly, using one hand to pull her hair out of her line of vision but still unable to see him.

"Yep."

"You can stop now."

That was the last thing he wanted to do. Beneath his hands Addy's flesh shone like gold dust in the campfire light. She had such a beautiful back—slim, shapely. He remembered that sprinkle of freckles across her shoulders. The softness of her skin invited kisses. He had to focus on the fact that he was supposed to be playing Good Samaritan here. But it was torture, touching her this way. Like a glimpse of hidden treasure that's out of reach.

"I haven't finished," he told her.

"That's all right."

"No, it's not." He ran a hand across her shoulder blades. "You're tighter than an over-wound pocket watch up here. And breathe, will you? It's very unflattering to have you act as if I'm getting ready to take a bite out of you."

For a moment she continued to lie tense. Then, as though testing release from intolerable pain, Addy expelled a long, cautious breath.

"That's better," David said. "Now relax. I'll have you know, it's been at least a month since I've forced my attentions on any unsuspecting injured women."

She murmured something, but he couldn't make it out. She was about to slip into sleep again.

Just as well, he thought.

He inhaled sharply as his chest tightened. It was a very good thing Addy couldn't see that his best intentions were critically close to dissolving into plain, American male lust. He swallowed hard and willed away desire with seemingly the last scrap of logic left to him. There were too many reasons why he couldn't give in to the demands of his body, not the least of which was Addy's vulnerable condition.

It might be easier to resist this woman if she was at least unconscious again. "Why don't you try to sleep?" he encouraged.

She must have heard the abruptness in his voice. She arched her neck as if she would look back at him. "I'm sorry this happened. I've never had a mishap like this before."

"It's all right. We'll manage. And when we get back, I want you to be sure to tell everyone how adept I was out here."

She nodded, then stifled a yawn. "I will. I promise." She slipped her hand back, wiggling her fingers. "David…?"

"Hmm?"

"I'm awfully glad you're the one who's out here with me."

He captured her hand, squeezing it lightly. "Me, too, Addy. Now get some rest."

She nodded again and closed her eyes. Very soon he heard her breathing settle, but it was a long time before he let go of her hand.

WHEN ADDY WOKE AGAIN, it was still dark and she could see the campfire's glowing embers a few feet away. David had used the sleeping bags to create a warm nest for her. It was especially nice since the temperature had dropped a little during the night.

He'd taken such good care of her. Seeing to her every need. Gentle and kind. A woman could get used to having him around.

Her headache was gone, but she was thirsty. She sat up, intent on finding the canteen David had placed beside her earlier. She moved cautiously, discovering that she wasn't nearly as sore as she had expected to be.

In the dim firelight she couldn't see the canteen, and when she stretched out her hand to hunt it down, she encountered a solid wall of bedding that turned out to be David. He was asleep beside her. As soon as her fingers stumbled over his chest, he jerked a little and sat up on one elbow.

"What is it?" he asked quickly, trying to find her eyes. "Are you all right?"

"I was looking for the canteen."

He reached behind him and handed it to her.

She took several deep swallows and gave it back. Then she lay down. Above she could see the Big Dipper. It looked so beautiful that she sighed.

"How's the head?" David asked.

"Fine."

"Can you go back to sleep?"

Her eyes now adjusted to the dark, she turned in his direction. "I could. But I don't want to."

"Can I get you anything?"

"No." She narrowed her eyes at him, trying to remember the hours she seemed to have lost. "Did you give me a back rub?"

"Yes. Want another one?"

"I don't think that would be a good idea."

He grinned. "No funny stuff, I promise. I'd only be checking for bruises."

"You might end up with a few of your own."

He made a face of mock disappointment. "Just when I thought I'd lulled you into a false sense of security."

She laughed and stared back at the sky. It felt nice to be here, close in the dark together. Warm. Intimate. Whatever their differences, right now they seemed so insignificant. "There's the North Star," she said. "Bright tonight."

"What else can you see?"

"Ursa Minor." She tilted her head. After a long moment she continued, "Scorpius."

"Still no Andromeda?"

"Afraid not," she told him. Her glance slid to his. "Poor Perseus. No princess waiting for her hero tonight."

"Maybe she's taking the night off to visit Earth," he speculated. His fingers reached across the distance that separated them and entwined with hers. He lifted them to his lips. Over their steepled grasp his smiling eyes looked directly into hers. "Think she'd settle for a mere mortal?"

She shook her head. "I don't know...princesses are notoriously picky."

"Well, mortals are notoriously persistent."

"You know those mythical maidens," she complained with a philosophic air. "Everything has to be pixie dust and magic. And love—all that silly stuff. Don't bother knocking on the old castle door if you're a guy who can't produce that happy ending."

His lips still pressed to her fingers, he brooded on her words. "The problem is, princess, I'm not sure I believe in happy endings anymore."

"Me, either," Addy said, though she knew in her heart that she loved David McKay, that she had always loved him and that she always would. Being with him now, it was like an emotional hurricane. And as much as she'd sworn never to put herself in that position again, she couldn't help it.

She wanted him.

CHAPTER THIRTEEN

SAM AND ROSE USUALLY ate dinner before the kitchen opened for the evening, but not tonight. Tonight two birthday celebrations the lodge catered had taken up all of their time, and Sam was relieved when the excitement was finally over and the kitchen closed. He and Rose had eaten late at the big wooden table, just the two of them. The hired help and the rest of the family had gone home. The place was quiet.

Rosa had hardly said a word all evening. When Sam had complimented her on her chicken Bianca, she hadn't even acknowledged that he'd spoken. Something was definitely bothering her.

"Here you go," Rosa said as she slid dessert in front of him.

He scowled down at the bowl, a quivering mass of green Jell-O.

"What's this?" he asked.

"Dessert," Rosa answered as she headed for the back counter, where she had been putting away her best knives.

"Dessert?" Sam jerked upright. That was impossible. No one ate Jell-O for dessert. This must be Rosa's idea of a joke. He surveyed the room, hoping to catch sight of the dessert tray. "Where's the cannolis?"

"We're out. I sent the last one to table four at lunch today."

"But you always save the last one for me."

"Not tonight," she said plainly. She motioned toward the dish in front of him with one of her knives. "Eat your Jell-O."

"I don't eat Jell-O," Sam replied, almost offended by the idea. "And certainly not when it's *green.*"

"I thought you loved it."

Sam looked at his wife as if she'd gone mad. "You know better than that."

Rosa tossed her knife into the drawer with a bang. That should have warned Sam that something was seriously wrong. Rosa was insane about her cutlery. She came to the table, and he saw that her eyes were flinty.

She stopped in front of him. "You certainly seemed to love it yesterday."

"What are you talking about?"

"Yesterday at the hospital. You took great pains to coax Geneva McKay to eat hers."

"I was trying to get her to eat something. I was just pretending to like it."

She tilted her head at him. God, he usually loved the way she did that. But when she spoke, her words shocked him right down to his socks. "Really? And what else are you pretending?"

Sam frowned. "Will you please stop talking in riddles?"

He was beginning to lose patience. Rosa was the most practical of women. This wasn't like her. And he didn't like it.

She gave him a scathing look, turned on her heel and marched through the double doors that led to the family's private quarters. Sam rose slowly, then followed her. What had gotten into Rosa? In all the years of their marriage he'd never seen her like this.

The living room was empty, so he made a beeline for their bedroom. He opened the door and immediately saw that his wife had taken up her usual seat at the vanity. She was brushing her hair so ferociously that he was amazed it wasn't coming out in handfuls.

He came up behind her, trying to find her eyes in the mirror. "Rosie, what's this all about? What's wrong?"

She shrugged his hands off her shoulders. "You tell me," she snapped. "You're the one making cow eyes at another woman!"

Her voice broke in two, like a piece of hard toffee. He stared at her for a long time, unable to believe what he'd just heard. Where would she get such an idea?

"What other woman?" he asked at last.

She swiveled on the bench seat, pointing at him with her brush. "Don't lie to me, Sam D'Angelo. I know something's going on between you and Geneva McKay."

Sam felt his face freeze in an expression of shock. "What! You can't be serious."

She narrowed her glare, clearly not believing him. "Then explain to me why you smelled of her perfume when you came to bed that first night she spent here. And why you're suddenly making secret calls in the kitchen pantry." She tossed her hairbrush on the vanity.

"Did you think I wouldn't figure it out?" she demanded. "I saw the looks you two were giving one another in the hospital." Her chin wobbled a little, and in his entire life Sam had never seen her look so miserable. "I might have piano legs and sagging breasts, but I am not stupid. I can see beyond my own nose."

He stared at her, a woman he didn't know at all any longer. "This is ridiculous. You think I'm having an affair with Geneva?"

"You deny it?"

"Of course I deny it. The woman is at least ten years older than I am."

"That doesn't matter. She's kept her figure. And she's a handsome woman. A man can decide to do mischief for a lot of foolish reasons."

Sam made a scoffing sound. "Not *this* man."

"So I've imagined all this? There's nothing going on between you?"

"Well…"

He stopped. The accusation of an affair was unthinkable, but telling Rosie the truth, that he and Geneva had been scheming to get their children back together, wouldn't win him any medals, either. How should he approach that?

Rosa evidently saw his hesitation as guilt. She made a move to slip off the bench and get past him. He grabbed her arms and settled her back down. "Now hold on, Rosie. Give me a chance to explain."

"There is no explanation for betrayal."

"Oh, yes, there is," Sam said, then frowned. "No, that's not what I mean. Damn it, you're getting me mixed up. Just sit and listen, will you?"

She was quiet for a time, nostrils flared, her features tight and suspicious. Finally she said, "One chance to explain. And it had better be good."

He had to smile at that. Really, it was so unlike Rosie to be jealous of anything. Especially another woman. Kind of nice to see that she could still be so territorial. "Or what?" he said with a gentle laugh. "You'll poison my Jell-O?"

She didn't laugh. She just stared at him. Hard. Sam swallowed, suddenly sensing that he'd better be pretty darned convincing.

IT WAS EARLY AFTERNOON when they rode onto Lightning River Lodge property, and in no time Addy was tying Sheba's reins to the hitching post in front of the stable. David slid wordlessly off Joe and began pulling one of the pack mules toward the rail.

In spite of the fact that they were both exhausted and she was a little sore from her fall, she had pushed them even harder the rest of the way back. She'd kept the breaks short, and they'd stopped for the night only after the last of a brilliant sunset had left the sky. Meals had been simple and uninspired, and she'd found an excuse to say good-night early instead of allowing them time for any more talk.

Tension began to stretch between them again, and Addy believed it was for the best anyway. They were almost done with one another—David would surely be on the first flight back to Los Angeles once he made sure his grandmother was all right.

And then that would be the end of it.

She glanced at David as she tied off Geneva's mount. "I know you must be eager to check on your grandmother. Don't bother with anything. I'll take care of this. You go ahead."

"This won't take long if we do it together."

"I do this all the time by myself. Go see Geneva. And tell her I'll be coming to see her soon."

He looked as if he might argue, but then grimaced. "You're still the trail boss."

"Right you are," Addy said. Before he could say anything more, she slipped Sheba's saddle off and headed for the tack room. Almost immediately she regretted that action. It seemed ungrateful and unfair somehow to leave it this way between them. After all, he was the man who had looked after her the night of her fall. Before she reached the barn door, she had to turn around.

David was walking toward the lodge.

"David," she called.

He swung back. With the saddle hitched against one hip, she came toward him.

"I just wanted to tell you..." She licked her lips and began again. "Thank you. When Sheba fell down that hill...I couldn't have managed that night without you."

"You're welcome. Always glad to help a lady in distress."

"After the accident I was kind of in a trance. Not myself, really. What I'm trying to say is—" the words caught in her throat for a moment before spilling out "—if I said or did anything I shouldn't have—"

"You didn't."

She swallowed her heart and nodded quickly. "Good."

He gave her a searching glance. "You've done an excellent job avoiding me the last two days. I'm going to see Gran now, but sooner or later you and I need to talk."

It was so difficult to sort through her chaotic thoughts when he said things like that. Her head reeling, she said, "You're not going to make this easy for me, are you?"

His lips curved into a sympathetic smile. In a softly textured voice he replied, "Whatever happens…I'd be willing to bet it won't be easy for either one of us."

She caught movement from the corner of her eye and saw Brandon coming down the path toward them. David saw him, too.

"Looks like help is on the way," he said. "I'll talk to you later."

DAVID ARRIVED IN HIS grandmother's hospital room to find her sitting on the side of her bed, arguing with her old friend Polly Swinburne. Her color was good. She was fully dressed, and as soon as she saw David, she beamed with obvious relief.

"There you are!" she exclaimed. "Just in time."

"In time for what?" he asked as he approached the hospital bed and nodded a greeting toward Polly.

"The doctor has released me. I can get out of here."

"Great! What does the doctor say?"

"I'm in tip-top shape." She accepted David's kiss on the cheek, then wrinkled her nose. "You smell like a horse, dear."

"I've missed you, too," he said with a light laugh. He was so relieved to see his grandmother looking more like her old self again. "I came straight here as soon as Addy and I got back."

"Everything went all right?" she asked, and he could see how eager she was for details. "You took care of…things?"

"Everything went fine. I'll tell you all about it when we're alone."

"And you and Addy?"

"We missed your company."

He knew that wasn't what she wanted to hear, and she wrinkled her nose at him.

Polly spoke up. "Talk some sense into her, David. The doctor says she should behave herself. I've told her she can stay with me, but she insists on going up to Lightning River Lodge for a few days."

His grandmother gave her friend a quelling look. "The D'Angelos have extended their hospitality to me. I see no reason not to take them up on it instead of imposing on you, Polly."

"Nonsense!" Polly complained. "How are you supposed to rest with all that foolishness going on up there?" To David she said, "There's some men's club reunion thing this weekend. It'll be chaos and too much excitement. A bunch of rowdy hooligan boys, no doubt."

Geneva scowled at her friend. "They're called SIX PAK, and it's no such thing. Sam said it was the reunion of six college students who have stayed friends for years. Their *twentieth* reunion, so I'd hardly expect them to be boys. But it does sound as though things will be hopping with them around."

Polly sniffed. "It sounds like nothing but booze and testosterone to me. I can't believe Rose would let Sam book a group like that. It's not a good place for you, Geneva."

"Oh, stop being melodramatic. It will be fine. Besides, I don't want to go home and just sit around taking my pulse and waiting for something to happen. I feel like being around people for a while."

"Then come and stay with me," Polly said. "*I'm* people."

When his grandmother cut a pleading look at David, he picked up on her thoughts immediately. She might like Polly, but twenty-four hours a day in her company was another matter. "I think staying up at the lodge will do you some good, Gran. I'll book a room, too. We can take walks by the lake or just sit out in the sunshine and catch up on old times."

"And when is she supposed to get rest?" Polly asked.

"*She* will make that decision," Gran answered. She turned back to David, looking confused. "But I thought you'd be leaving for

Los Angeles as soon as the trip was over. Don't you have business to attend to?"

"As a matter of fact, I do. I won't be able to spend more than a few days. But I'd like to spend them here with you, Gran."

His grandmother sat up straighter and gave him a narrowed glance. "Does that mean—"

He cut her off by laying his hand upon her shoulder. He knew what she wanted to hear—that he and Addy had somehow formed a new bond—but he couldn't give her that. If anything, they seemed to have drifted further apart than ever. "It *means* that I want to spend as much time as I can with you before I have to go. That's all."

She subsided with a disappointed sigh.

Polly wagged a finger in her friend's direction. "Mark my words, this is a mistake. Lightning River Lodge is not the place for peace and quiet this weekend."

"Good," Geneva said firmly. "Because there will be plenty of time for peace and quiet when I'm in my grave."

THAT AFTERNOON DAVID and his grandmother took adjoining rooms on the second floor of the lodge.

Gran seemed to glow with excitement, and as David settled her suitcase on the bed, she went immediately to the balcony doors and threw them wide.

"Oh, David, come look at the view!"

David barely glanced up. "I've seen it before, Gran."

"Well, come look anyway. It's so lovely."

He followed her out onto the balcony. "Very nice," he said automatically and then stopped, because the view really was awe-inspiring and it seemed to go on forever. Ridge upon ridge of high peaks in the distance, and Lightning Lake shining like a sliver of mirror.

"Admit it," his grandmother said. "You can't get this kind of air in Hollywood."

David inhaled deeply of the crisp afternoon breeze. It was so pure it stung his nostrils. "You're right," he admitted. "Unfortunately I can't make a living up here."

"You could if you decided to do something else with your life."

He lowered a eyebrow at her, an unspoken warning not to give him grief about his career. She didn't really need to anyway. In the last week or so he'd started to think a lot about his past decisions. Sometimes lately he'd even begun to wonder why he'd made them.

"All right," his grandmother said. "So you can't be a big-time producer up here. At least tell me the last time you took a vacation."

He looked at his watch. "Just got back from one three hours and thirty-seven minutes ago."

"That wasn't a vacation. That was just a duty you thought you owed to me. When before that?"

He actually had to stop and think about his answer. He'd traveled the world over several times but couldn't for the life of him remember the last time he'd done it for pleasure. He never made his own reservations anymore, never spent much time seeing the sights. For the past few years travel had been strictly business. Vacations were for the people who worked for him.

He shrugged. "I can't remember."

"You see? You're a workaholic. Somewhere along the way you've forgotten how to relax and enjoy yourself."

That was probably true. He'd recaptured a little of that feeling out on the trail with Addy and his grandmother. That sense that the world would keep revolving just fine without him.

But it couldn't last. He still had a production company to run and he'd already lost valuable time. His assistant had proved that he could juggle projects well, and now that David was linked to the office once more, some of the hiccups were ironing out. But in a matter of days he had to be back in Los Angeles. He *had* to. That was just the way it was.

Wasn't it?

Geneva cleared her throat. "And since you won't volunteer any information, I'll just come right out and ask. Where do you and Addy really stand with one another?"

"Right where we used to," David said. He spread his hands wide. "About a million miles apart."

"And that's the way you want it?"

"That's the way it is."

"Well, it doesn't have to be. You could—"

He ducked his head and gave his grandmother a quelling frown. "Gran, stop. I've cleared my calendar to give us another couple of days together. Do you intend to spend the entire time lecturing me about my lifestyle and love life?"

"Yes," she said unexpectedly. "Whatever it takes."

David shook his head and turned back into the bedroom. "It won't do you any good."

"Can't do me any harm, either," he heard her mutter as she walked farther out onto the balcony.

THAT EVENING THE LODGE sponsored a wine-and-cheese party for its guests. David escorted his grandmother down to the library, where the gathering was already spilling out into the lobby. It was a festive event, with plenty of good wine flowing amid lots of laughter. There were three or four couples present, as well as most of the D'Angelos. David had no more handed his grandmother a glass of ginger ale than several of them came over to say hello.

He realized that Addy's family had grown considerably since he'd left Broken Yoke. There were aunts and grandchildren and new wives, and everyone seemed eager to make the evening a success for the family business.

His eyes immediately sought out Addy and found her standing in a back corner, surrounded by a group of men. David assumed it was the reunion group Polly Swinburne had been so worried about—SIX PAK.

Her prediction of a wild bunch seemed unfounded. The men all looked respectable, friendly and in the prime of middle age.

"Addy seems to have made new friends," his grandmother pointed out as her glance turned toward the corner, as well.

"Good for her," David replied as he swallowed a sip of wine.

He wasn't surprised by all the attention Addy had attracted. She was a beautiful woman, moving with elegance even in freshly pressed jeans and a suede jacket the color of dark honey. Her thick, silky hair spilled freely down her back, hair a man could wrap around his hands and get lost in.

The SIX PAK guys seemed charmed by her presence, particularly one tall jock type with prematurely graying hair and a rugged face. Not incredibly handsome but enough to catch a woman's notice. Where was O'Dell? David wondered. Shouldn't he be here guarding his territory? But he wasn't in the room or manning the front desk.

Suddenly he felt the need to check out some of the books on the shelves of the D'Angelos' well-stocked library. Particularly those in that back corner.

He left his grandmother chatting with Kari, Nick D'Angelo's wife, and headed across the room. As he approached the group and they became aware of his arrival, Addy turned. She looked a little surprised to see him, and in the depths of her eyes he glimpsed a sudden wariness. Her chin had risen as though in preparation for battle.

"Hello, Addy," David said. "Mind if I join you?"

He suspected she did, but she could hardly say so. Polite, weak smiles passed between them, and the men around her began to introduce themselves.

As it turned out, SIX PAK wasn't the name they'd given their group because of a predilection for beer or frat parties. One of them explained that it stood for Steven,

Ian, Alex, Paul, Anthony and Kyle—their first names.

"Makes sense, I suppose," David said. "But who's the X in SIX PAK?"

The one who had introduced himself as Alex, the gray-haired jock, lifted his hand. "That's me. We already had an *A*—Anthony here. So I got stuck being the *X*. For Alexander." He grinned sheepishly. "It seemed like a good idea at the time, but twenty years later it's a little embarrassing to have these bozos still referring to me as X-Man."

Paul grunted. "Back then we thought we were tough, clever hombres." He patted his stomach, which looked as if it had a good relationship with pizza and fast foods. "For a week every year we get to pretend we're twenty-one again, but the rest of the time we accept the fact that we're just a bunch of guys with receding hairlines and bad knees."

The men laughed good-naturedly at that description.

Paul tossed a glance at Addy. "I hope you're going to take it easy on us, Miss D'Angelo."

When David gave Addy a curious look, she

spoke up. "I'm taking SIX PAK out on an over-night camping trip the day after tomorrow."

This time it was David who could barely suppress his surprise. For a moment he felt entirely separate from the rest of the group, caught in his own web of apprehension, dis-approval and...jealousy.   Unexpected jealousy. He knew he had no right to object. No right at all. He was too old for it. Too mature. But it was there all the same.

Of course, he was sensible enough to know he had to grit his teeth and swallow any ob-jection. Instead he smiled at the group. "You'll be in good hands," he told them. "Addy is a very competent trail boss. Just be sure you do your share or she'll send you home."

The men laughed again and made promises to behave. He watched them try to charm Addy, jockeying for attention, and felt a pinch of resentment that she didn't seem to mind.

David didn't know how many of these guys were married, but Alex, the gray-haired stud, wasn't wearing a wedding ring. He seemed particularly interested in making points with Addy—leaning closer for greater intimacy, little touches at the elbow, a broad laugh that revealed teeth whiter than peppermint Chiclets.

It was annoying as hell, and David had no idea where that irritation came from. No place near where his common sense originated. Disgusted with himself, he forced a cool mantel of control to come down over his features, excused himself from the group and went off in search of better company.

CHAPTER FOURTEEN

THE PARTY WAS STILL going strong when Addy left the lodge and headed for her favorite place of refuge—the stable.

She was annoyed with the whole universe, most of all herself. She'd stayed longer at the party than she'd wanted to simply because it had seemed like the sensible thing to do.

Meet new people. Put the fantasies away. Get on with life.

She'd chatted and laughed and pretended interest where there really was none. She'd met some nice people, even flirted a little with one of the men in the reunion group. And still loneliness had covered her like a heavy cloak. It blocked out everything. Everyone.

Except David.

Why couldn't he go back where he belonged? She was ready to start phase one of her new life. This afternoon, seeing no reason to delay, she'd called the sperm bank in Denver to make an appointment for next week.

She'd also talked to Brandon about their relationship. She cared deeply about him, but it could never be more than friendship. If he could accept that, she'd still like to partner with him at the stable. If she was lucky enough to get pregnant right away, she'd need all the help she could get.

He'd been surprisingly understanding about her decision, but her mood hadn't lightened much.

She let herself into the tack room, determined to take her mind off everything with the only remedy she knew—hard work. She removed her jacket and concentrated on repairing a bridle, reworking the leather again and again until she was completely satisfied. She had the SIX PAK trip ahead of her, a job sure to keep her on her toes, and preparation always paid off.

She had just finished rebraiding reins for Sheba's lead rope when she heard the door open behind her. She turned, hoping it wasn't a guest in search of conversation. She wasn't feeling particularly sociable right now.

Unfortunately it *was* a guest, though when she saw which one, she couldn't honestly say she minded that much. It was Alex Hutchinson, one of the SIX PAK group. She had liked him almost immediately. That premature gray hair was deceiving—he had a youthful laugh and a twinkle in his eyes that went along with a voice that had disc-jockey depth.

"Hi," she greeted him. "Out for a walk?"

"Not really. I was looking for you and one of your brothers said you might be down here. Since you left the party early, should I assume you prefer the company of horses rather than people?"

"Depends on the people."

"How about me?" he asked lightly. "Should I leave?"

His eyes were so blue and candid that Addy found herself smiling. "I think you can stay." She patted a nearby bale of hay. "Have a seat. You can keep me company while I work."

He settled on a bale, cocking one leg over

his knee. He watched her hands weave the leather, to the point where she began to feel self-conscious of his scrutiny. Why had he sought her out? Boredom? Or attraction? The thought made her stomach feel as if it were filled with netted butterflies.

But gradually Addy began to relax in his company. He asked questions, showed an interest, and for about an hour they talked of inconsequential things. She learned that he was in his early forties—though he certainly didn't look it—and was a fairly successful nature photographer who lived in Maine with a daughter from a previous marriage.

When he slipped off the bale of hay as though he intended to call it a night, Addy was almost sorry to see him go. Who said she could only be truly happy in a man's company if that man was David?

Alex picked a bit of hay from his sleeve. "I understand that in addition to everything else you do around here you're also a licensed helicopter pilot."

Addy nodded. "My brother Nick is the head of Angel Air, but I help out when he needs it."

"Could I hire Angel Air to take me up tomorrow morning?"

"You want to do the tourist thing?"

"Not exactly. I've heard that the National Park Service has reintroduced elk to Wilderness Valley. I'd like to get a few pictures if I can."

"I'll check with Nick when I go back up to the lodge. I'm sure he can help you."

His mouth quirked into a grin. "I was thinking that I might convince *you* to take me."

Addy stopped what she was doing and looked at him closely. "Why me?"

"Because I think you'd be good company. And because I find you attractive and interesting to talk to. Do I need more reasons than that?"

A long note of silence passed between them. Finally she said, "I suppose not."

Alex frowned, then tilted his head at her. "I'm sorry, I should have asked. Are you... seeing someone?"

She wanted so badly to say yes. She wanted to tell this nice, handsome man that he was wasting his time. But she couldn't, of course, and the dream left her, skittering behind a closing door. "Not really," she said at last.

"But...?"

Should she tell him about her plans for a baby? Almost immediately she decided against it. This man wasn't offering a lifetime commitment. He was only looking for a date. "But nothing," she said with a smile. "No, I'm not seeing anyone."

"Good. Then can we get an early start tomorrow morning? I promised the fellows I'd meet up with them by noon."

"How's seven?"

"Fine. I'll be in the lobby by seven. I think we'll have fun. Don't you?"

"Yes," she said, though she knew she sounded too brisk, too insincere. She softened her tone. "Yes, I think we'll have a great time."

BY SEVEN THE NEXT DAY Sam had already been up for hours. He liked the clean charm of the morning best, and because so many of the area's activities required an early start, he could visit with many of the guests on their way outdoors. He stood behind the front desk, checking the night auditor's work and smiling as guests headed for the dining room. Overhead he heard the creak of pine floors and the occasional sound of a door closing, the lodge coming awake to greet a new day.

Rosa came out to join him. As usual, she carried a plate of blueberry muffins, which she placed on one of the lobby tables next to the complimentary-coffee station. He watched her work, a vision of efficiency. So what if she had a little extra on her hips? His wife looked like an angel in that tube of sunlight coming in through the tall windows.

He was glad they'd gotten all that nonsense about Geneva McKay behind them. It had taken some convincing, but Rosa had believed him in the end, and that was all that mattered.

Unfortunately she'd wrung an unwilling promise out of him, as well. He must stop trying to fix Addy up with David. Butt out, she'd said firmly. And tell Geneva to stop interfering, too.

He had sworn to her that he would. But it had certainly taken the fun out of things.

"One of those muffins for me?" Sam called across the lobby.

Rosa didn't even turn to look at him. "No."

Sam made a face. "I'm stuck behind the desk until George comes at noon. A person could starve by then."

"You won't."

"Nice to be appreciated around here," Sam grumbled.

Rosa ignored him and continued tidying the coffee station. In a bad mood, he supposed. He sighed dramatically so she could hear him and went back to checking yesterday's receipts.

In a few minutes his sister-in-law Renata came out of the dining room carrying a covered tray. Instead of heading upstairs, she plopped it down on the front desk counter. When she lifted the lids, Sam saw his favorite breakfast— pancakes dripping with warm syrup and one egg slightly scrambled and dotted with cheese.

"What's this?" Sam asked.

Renata looked as though she'd been sucking on lemons. "Rose says if we don't feed you breakfast you'll be a bear all day." She glanced back over her shoulder at her sister. "*I* say, how would that be different from any other day? But it's her kitchen."

With that, she turned on her heel and marched back toward the dining room. Renata had a wasp's tongue sometimes, but Sam knew that she loved being here at the lodge, and she ran the kitchen like a field marshal.

Sam looked at his wife, and almost by instinct, she glanced back over her shoulder and smiled at him. He returned it. They had been made for each other from the very beginning and they both had known it. Rosa was his soul mate, and it was good to have her back now that she'd decided to forgive him.

He took a forkful of pancakes and was about to offer Rosa some when he heard movement on the stairs. Alex Hutchinson.

Sam was surprised. Knowing they'd had a late night of conversation and drinks in the library, he wasn't expecting to see any of the SIX PAK group up and out so early. But the guy seemed ready to go somewhere, dressed casually in jeans and a polo shirt. Over one shoulder he carried a massive camera bag.

Sam grinned at the man. "You're up early! Where are you fellows headed today?"

"The others are sleeping in. We're driving up to Mount Evans after lunch." He tapped his camera case. "But first I'm going to take some pictures."

"Good morning for it," Sam said, putting down his fork and sliding effortlessly into genial-host mode. "Need a map or directions?"

"Actually I'm taking one of your helicopters out to Wilderness Valley. I'm hoping to catch sight of a few elk."

Sam nodded. Since the Park Service had moved some of the elk into that valley, there had been a lot of interest. Maybe it was time to mention it in the lodge's brochure. He'd talk to Nick today about officially adding a tour or two.

He chatted with Hutchinson for a few more minutes and watched as the man took out his camera and fiddled with the settings. In the meantime, David McKay came downstairs. His hair was furrowed as though he'd driven his fingers through it instead of a comb, and a day-old growth of beard shadowed his cheeks.

Though Sam had sworn to behave, he

couldn't help thinking that Adriana would love to see him like this. Much to Sam's chagrin, his daughter had never been interested in the three-piece-suit kind of guy. She seemed to prefer the scruffy sort.

Sam and Hutchinson greeted David as he came over to the front desk, and after David had returned their greeting, he held up his electric shaver. "I don't suppose you have any extra batteries lying around?"

"Sure do," Sam said. "Let me get them from the back office." He turned toward Hutchinson. "You have fun out there. And don't you worry. Nick will make sure you find some elk."

Hutchinson shook his head. "Your son isn't flying me to Wilderness Valley. Your daughter is."

Sam stopped dead in his tracks. "Adriana?"

Hutchinson chuckled. "Do you have another daughter?"

"No, no." Sam waved away that query, still not certain he'd heard correctly. "Addy's taking you up?"

"Yes. I asked her last night."

When exactly had this happened? Addy wasn't supposed to be making new male friends. She was supposed to be finding interest in the old ones. "But—"

The front door opened and Addy breezed in. She looked lovely this morning, hair down and shining, her cheeks pink with excitement. "Good morning, everyone!" she said as she came toward them. She gave Hutchinson an apologetic smile. "I'm sorry I'm a little late. I was down at the hangar. All ready to go?"

"Yes," the man said. "Looking forward to it."

Sam had noticed a few other things about Adriana, too. Like a little more makeup around his daughter's eyes and the fact that she wasn't dressed in the practical jumpsuit she usually wore when she took tourists up. She looked as though she'd taken a little extra time with her outfit this morning—a fresh pair of slacks and a red blouse that hugged her upper body more than Sam liked.

He watched Addy and Hutchinson talk a few moments. He knew that look in her eyes. That reckless, saucy quirk of her lips.

What did David McKay think about all this?

Sam slid a glance toward David, only to discover him perusing the front page of the Denver newspaper that lay on top of the counter. Sam barely hid a growl of impatience. What was wrong with the man? *Wake up,* cafone! Sam wanted to shout. *Can't you see what's going on right under your nose?*

Well, if McKay didn't have sense enough to do something, Sam certainly did. Before Addy and Hutchinson could trot out the door, he turned toward his daughter, giving her a serious look. "Adriana, did you talk this trip over with Nick?"

Addy was taken by surprise. "I don't need to. There's no one else booked and Nick knows I know the drill."

That was certainly true. Perhaps a different approach. "I thought you wanted my help this morning with that broken stall door."

"That can wait until this afternoon." Addy turned back to Alex Hutchinson, reaching out to run a finger along his camera. "That's a very impressive camera."

The giveaway sparkle of anticipation was in the man's eyes. "If you can find those elk," he said in a low voice, "I'll show you how to use it."

"I'd like that," Addy said sweetly. "Shall we go?"

Desperate, Sam raised his hand. "Wait!" He turned toward his guest. "Mr. Hutchinson, it might be better if you let Nick take you up. He's much more experienced than Adriana. He flew helicopters in the service. In the war."

Addy gasped. "What a thing to say!" Indignation was written clearly on her features. After giving Sam one long glare of annoyance, she turned back to Hutchinson. "My brother *is* more experienced, but I've been flying for quite a while. And since we aren't likely *to be shot at*..." she added with a meaningful look toward her father.

"Did she tell you that she once crashed one of our helicopters?" Sam blurted out. "Knocked the struts clean off and had to be taken to the hospital along with one of our guests."

"Pop!"

Addy's gaze clashed with Sam's. Across the room he glimpsed Rosa turning to look at him. He could see that his wife had heard everything and wasn't liking a bit of it.

Unexpectedly David McKay spoke up. *Finally,* thought Sam. "It's just my opinion, but I think Addy is one of the most capable people I've ever met." He inclined his head toward Sam. "No offense to your son, Mr. D'Angelo, but I can't imagine anyone better than Addy as Mr. Hutchinson's pilot." He smiled at the man. "She's also an excellent guide and will give you a great appreciation for this area."

"Great," Alex said, then glanced Addy's way. "Just talking to you last night, I'm half in love with this place already."

Sam stood there feeling helpless and furious with David McKay. Why was he encouraging this outing? Someone else had to be doing the driving for this boy. Addy and this Hutchinson fellow out in the wilderness alone together? All that scenic beauty. The warmth of the sun that would send the temperature of desire soaring impossibly. Was McKay blind to what was brewing here?

"I think…" Sam began, but in that moment he caught sight of his wife giving him the hard eye. He had to back off. A promise was a promise, and Rosa wasn't likely to be sending him anymore pancakes if he broke it so quickly.

And then he realized in that moment that, with or without his vow not to interfere, he couldn't continue to matchmake for Addy. Rosa had always been wiser than him in matters of the heart. She had faith in their children. She had faith in love.

If it was meant to be, David and Addy would find a way.

He touched Addy's arm, feeling her stiffen slightly beneath his fingers. "My apologies, daughter," he said in a calm, conciliatory voice. "You're an excellent pilot, and Mr. Hutchinson will have a wonderful time."

She gave him a little smile, then took Hutchinson's arm. Sam watched them go.

Then he went to get the batteries for David McKay's razor, grumbling all the way. Love was very frustrating. And no doubt his pancakes were stone-cold.

ADDY DELIVERED ALEX back to the lodge's front door just before noon. The rest of the

SIX PAK group was already on the front porch, waiting for him. As soon as Addy pulled up in the company Jeep, Alex gathered his camera case and leaned over to give her a kiss on the cheek.

"Your father was right," he said. "I had a terrific time. And I'm glad we didn't crash."

Addy laughed and shook her head. "I don't know what gets into my father sometimes."

"I think I understand it. When my own daughter grows up, I'm probably going to feel the same way."

"What way is that?"

A sharp whistle came from the porch. "Come on, X-Man," Paul called. "You're holding up the wagon train."

"Gotta run," Alex said with a grimace.

With a final goodbye, Addy watched Alex join his friends. Then the six men headed off to the parking lot. The tallest of the group, Alex was easy to keep track of; that silvery hair gleamed in the sunlight. He was a good-looking man. A nice guy. What woman wouldn't be glad to find someone like that interested in her?

Me.

Addy parked the Jeep in its usual spot, slung her backpack over her shoulder and entered the lodge. She went through the lobby, the dining room and the kitchen in silence, then through the double doors that led to their private quarters. She passed Rafe and Dani kissing on the couch. Rafe hardly looked up.

Dani, however, pulled away long enough to ask, "How did it go?"

"Fine," Addy replied and kept walking.

When she reached her room, she tossed her pack in a corner, toed off her shoes and fell on her bed. She lay on her back, hands pillowed under her head, staring at the ceiling. She felt completely drained, as though everything inside her had been sucked down into a black hole. She felt miserable.

And it was absolutely a misery of her own making.

This morning with Alex Hutchinson should have been great.

Because of his work, Alex had been in a helicopter many times and hadn't needed much instruction. They'd lifted off quickly, and the trip out to Wilderness Valley had begun in awkward silence. But that hadn't lasted long.

After that disastrous beginning in the lobby that morning, Addy had still been trying to absorb the fact that her father had deliberately tried to sabotage her, when Alex had tapped her arm. She'd turned her head to find him smiling at her.

"Don't let your father's words spoil this day," she'd heard him say through her headphones. "Let's enjoy this."

It had gotten easier then. Alex was a fun companion. He loved his work and he didn't mind answering questions as long as she was willing to share answers of her own. His interest could have gone straight to her head. He made no pretense of indifference. It was flattering and left her trying to find her equilibrium.

They'd found the elk. A small herd of does with a huge buck watching over them. After Alex had taken all the pictures he wanted, he had come back to the boulder where Addy had waited and settled beside her, his hair mussed attractively, a satisfied light in his eyes.

He had kissed her.

Confidently but gently. His lips had been warm and inviting, and Addy had realized she'd been waiting for a miracle there on that rock, waiting for her veins to run with fire, waiting for something to erupt in her again so that she might forget how much a crater her heart had become.

But it hadn't happened. And Alex Hutchinson had known it immediately.

He'd drawn back from her, tilting his head at her as he'd offered a small smile. "You lied to me last night, didn't you?"

"I don't know what you mean."

"I asked if you were seeing someone. You said no."

"I'm not," Addy had replied with a quick shake of her head. It had been embarrassing to have this man look at her as though he could read her soul. "I'm completely available. I'll let you look at my date book. It's blank. A clean slate."

He'd grinned. "But not your mind." He'd touched the front of her blouse lightly.

"Not your heart. Whoever he is, he's a lucky guy."

"Alex—"

He'd fallen away from her then, scooping up his camera. "It's all right, Addy. Now why don't you take me to this waterfall you were talking about earlier so we can both settle into friendship?"

Addy had watched Alex's retreating back, tall and resolute, as he'd headed for the helicopter. And that had been the end of it.

She punched her pillow higher and closed her eyes. The rest of the morning with Alex played out in her head. Full of good humor and an easy camaraderie.

But no sparks.

Not a one.

CHAPTER FIFTEEN

ADDY HEARD A SOFT TAP on her bedroom door and groaned inwardly. She wasn't in the mood for conversation, but there was always very little privacy in the D'Angelo household. She'd never minded that much in the past, but how would she manage if there was a baby in her life? She should talk to Rafe, maybe revisit his suggestion that she buy one of the condos he owned in downtown Broken Yoke.

Her sister-in-law Dani opened the door and poked her head around the edge. "Well? Can I come in?"

"I suppose, but don't expect chitchat."

Dani laughed and pushed the door wide. Behind her were Addy's other sisters-in-law, Kari and Leslie. After they had married her brothers, she'd come to care about all three of them, but the unexpectedness of this group visit made Addy's heart stall.

She sat up. Had something happened while she'd been out? "What's wrong?" she asked quickly.

"Nothing," Leslie said. "We just felt like getting away for a few minutes, so we thought we'd keep you company."

When Addy frowned at that, Dani made a scoffing sound. "Oh, baloney. I knew you wouldn't believe that. We actually came because we want to talk to you in private."

"About what?"

Dani settled against Addy's desk, and the other two women soon found places to perch, as well. "Pop told us about you taking one of the SIX PAK guys up this morning. How did it go?"

"I told you. Fine. Alex got lots of pictures."

"That's not what I meant. Rafe said that guy was all over you last night, trying to make points. So? How was it? Did you two hit it off out there?"

"Yes," Addy said, preferring to be deliberately obtuse. "I think Alex is going to be a good friend."

"I didn't know you needed any more friends," Dani complained.

Kari spoke up. "Are you supposed to take the SIX PAK group out on an overnight camping trip tomorrow?"

Addy settled back on her elbow. "Uh-huh. Rafe's going to help out. We're taking them out to Rainbow Falls." Addy looked at each of them. "What's this all about?"

There was a long silence and then Dani cleared her throat. "I guess you could call this an intervention of sorts."

Addy raised an eyebrow, intrigued. "I know I was knocking back more wine than I probably should have last night, but I don't think that indicates I have a drinking problem."

None of the women even cracked a smile. Something more serious was clearly on their minds. "Is this about my baby plans again?" she asked. "Because I haven't changed my mind."

"That's not what we're talking about," Dani replied. She nodded toward Kari and Leslie. "We've discussed your situation and we think it's time you faced your problem head-on."

"What situation? What problem?"

Dani drew a deep breath. "We think that as long as David McKay is staying at the lodge, you should stick around, too. Let Rafe take the SIX PAK guys out. He can manage it alone."

"And why would I do that?" Addy asked, beginning to lose patience at the unexpected mention of David's name.

No one said a thing for another long moment. Then Dani said, "Because you're in love with David, and we think he feels the same."

Addy straightened, pushing her hands outward to express her displeasure. "Hold it! Enough! I love you all, but you're interfering where you're not wanted. My love life is strictly my own business."

Kari laughed. "Why? You certainly had advice for us when *we* needed it. Now it's your turn. But we can't help you if you run away."

"I'm not running away. I have a job to do."

"You're just finding an excuse to avoid him," Kari continued. "I recognize that behavior when I see it because it's the same way I was with Nick. But we've all agreed—if you hide what you feel, if you try to make it go away, you'll only make yourself more crazy. A person you can't live without is like another form of oxygen. You need it. You need *him*."

There was an echoing silence. Addy scowled at them so long that Leslie stood and clutched her arm. "Addy, listen to us. David's grandmother says he's only going to be here through the weekend. Please don't let this opportunity slip through your fingers. I nearly lost Matt because I was afraid to take a chance, but the truth is, I just wasted precious time we could have had together."

Addy's skull felt as if it were made of glass. She rubbed her temples, feeling like a child who doesn't understand her scolding and only resents it. She knew these women meant well, but they didn't understand.

"What do you expect me to do?" Addy asked with a touch of belligerence. "Throw myself at David's feet and beg him to have his way with me?"

"So what if you did?" Kari asked. "What's wrong with that? And who knows where it might lead?"

Addy shook her head. "*I* know where it might lead. Disaster."

"Or maybe the two of you will discover a way to make the relationship work. You'll never know unless you give it a try."

"Have you completely forgotten that I want to have a baby in my life?" Addy said more vehemently. "Soon. I'm pretty sure David isn't thinking along those lines. It's a complication he doesn't need or want."

"Have you asked him?" Leslie spoke up.

"No, but—" Frustrated, Addy broke off, then took a different approach. "You just don't understand. If I let David back into my life, even temporarily, I'll never—" She looked at all the women in turn. They had become her dearest friends. She knew they cared about her. She knew she could put her greatest hopes and fears into words. "I *do* love David. But I'm afraid we might ruin it again. I don't want to be hurt."

She turned her back on them because she could feel the tears in her throat, tears that had gotten beyond her control at last. She dropped her face into her hands. It was so quiet in the bedroom.

Finally she felt an arm slip around her shoulders. It was Leslie, who had known her the longest, who had helped Addy in those first few days after she had miscarried David's baby.

Leslie drew Addy closer. "Sweetie, I know you don't want to be hurt," she said in the soft, gentle voice she probably used as a nurse. "But in spite of all the ways you think you've managed to put it behind you, somewhere deep inside, haven't you been hurting all these years?" She smiled. "I know how scary it is. But sometimes you just have to take a chance and see what happens."

"Leslie—"

Her sister-in-law stepped away and headed for the door. "Come on, ladies. We've done as much as we can without being labeled busybodies forever. Addy will decide what she wants to do." She looked back at Addy. "No matter what that decision is, you know we'll support you."

ALMOST AN HOUR LATER Addy walked out of her bedroom.

It was early in the afternoon. There was

still a full day of work ahead of her, a camping trip to prepare for, but she didn't head for the stable. She passed a few guests on their way outdoors. From the side porch she heard male laughter and then a muffled giddy response—the honeymooners finding a private moment.

Once in the lobby, she made a turn toward the stairs to the second floor. She took them slowly, her thoughts chaotic. She had made a decision. A frightening one. But she was determined to see it through. Inside she might be insecure and fearful, but those anxieties had dogged her long enough. It was time to chase them off once and for all.

Driven by a desire bigger than herself, she approached David's guest room door and knocked sharply before she could chicken out.

There was no answer. Ironic, wasn't it, that the moment she had finally made a move to do something definitive about their relationship, David appeared to be missing?

She stood there for a solid minute. All that determination boiling within her and no place to put it. She considered checking to see if he was keeping Geneva company in her room, then decided against it. Still, it was frustrating. What if he was passing time with his grandmother when he should be out here, talking to her?

She moved to Geneva's door and placed her ear against it. No sound at all from inside. Darn Pop for constructing the lodge with such great soundproofing.

Now what? Should she go back downstairs and forget the whole thing? Or camp out and wait for David to return? But suppose he was out for the day? Suppose he'd gone down to Denver, looking for more excitement? Suppose he'd made a new friend? The female kind.

"Looking for someone?" a male voice asked behind her, and Addy jumped guiltily and swung around.

David was coming up the stairs.

Addy gave him a wobbly smile, feeling foolish. "I was just checking to see…to see what you were up to."

"Gran's out by the lake with Polly Swin-burne."

"Oh. Well, I guess I don't need to worry

then. What about you? Are you having a good time? Or counting the minutes until you can catch your plane?"

He came slowly toward her, a quizzical look on his face. "Why are you here, Addy? Gran's trip is over. I've acknowledged that you knew what you were doing out there. I've thanked you. You've thanked me. In a very short time, both our lives are going to go back to the way they were. What's left to take care of between us?"

"Not much, I suppose. Except…one thing. I want you to kiss me. Please?"

She stared at him, watching the ropy muscles of his bared forearms tighten as he crossed his arms over his chest. She witnessed the strong workings of his throat.

Into the sudden uncomfortable silence she said, "I'm serious. Kiss me. Right now."

"Addy, don't play—"

"I'm not playing."

"Where's O'Dell? Or your silver-haired stud? If you're looking for distraction, I think he'd be willing to give it to you."

"I told Brandon yesterday that it wouldn't work between us. As for Alex, he's with his buddies. But I'm not looking for distraction from him. I'm coming to you because this may be the only chance we have before you leave. There may never be another one— ever. So if this is all we may get, I want you to kiss me. I want you to take me to bed. I want it. Please tell me you still want it, too."

His movements had frozen. The hall lighting threw sharp shadows upward on his rugged features, but in his eyes she read longing and so much more. He brought his fingers to her chin until their gazes met. Seconds ticked away while his eyes searched hers. They narrowed as he frowned.

"Addy, you can't know… Those days on the trail… Do you think I've enjoyed cursing the hours before sunrise, when I imagined you getting dressed in the tent and wondered what it would be like to see you naked in a new dawn? I know the scent of you and the way your footsteps sound and the path your hair will take down your back when you set it free at the end of the day. I know so many things about you and yet almost nothing at all. But I still want you. I've never stopped wanting you. Watching Alex Hutchinson with you this morning, do you know how much I wanted to go all caveman on his ass?"

"You didn't seem a bit bothered."

"You needed someone on your side against your father's manipulations." He touched her face lightly. "But I hated the idea of you going out into the wilderness with him. Or anyone else. I want you to stay here and be with me."

"Then show me why I should. Kiss me." Her heart knew before her head what she meant to do. She pressed her hand against his chest, feeling his heartbeat sprint against her fingers. Lifting her chin, she found his eyes. "Just kiss me as if you mean it."

Surprise flitted through his features, and then something seemed to relax in him— like an overcoiled spring suddenly released. With a sound somewhere between a growl and a purr he pulled her closer. "I've always meant it with you, Addy. Always."

He brushed his mouth against her temple, as though yielding to the burden of fate. Then whatever else he might have intended to say was lost as he lowered his head and his mouth connected with hers. His touch was featherlight and yet it jolted through Addy like an electric charge. A soft groan escaped her when he slipped his tongue into her mouth.

Things swept into a blur then, because David was there, touching her in places she had never dreamed could feel any more alive. As though aware that anyone might come up the stairs and see them, he fumbled with his room key, rammed it into the lock and got the door open. His hands pulled her blouse over her head even as he was closing the door behind them.

He had her naked quickly and laid her gently on the bed. There was no time to feel chilled. His lips were on her breasts. He began to play there eloquently, letting his tongue pour over her like spring sunshine, warm and delicate, until she was limp and pliant in his hold.

Beneath the curtain of her lashes she glimpsed his taut longing, and with the certainty of his desire for her, her body arched upward to meet every touch. His hands moved over her, and when his fingers slid between her legs, she knew she would accept his lovemaking without reservation, without regrets.

She moaned with anticipation and eagerness, and David's bright, consuming gaze sought hers. "Addy." His breath came hot against her cheek. "Are you sure? My God, this feels like summer madness."

"David—" She tugged back on his hair, meeting his hazy glance with wide, defiant eyes, because she didn't care what happened to her now. It was too late. Too late for anything but the fulfillment they both wanted and needed so desperately.

She rushed into speech, fearful only that he might end this. "I don't care. Don't stop," she murmured. "Don't you dare stop."

She read amusement in his eyes, and her lashes drifted down as a smile teased her mouth. She knew that her body pleased him, that she was well prepared to meet his need with her own. She listened to his ragged, impassioned breathing, self-conscious about her own passion and yet thrilled by it, as well. His hands knew how to court and enchant her body, as though no years had ever come between them.

His fingers probed lightly, deeper. She could feel control slipping out from under her. There was a kind of delicious tension between them now, and her eyes wouldn't be coaxed from his.

When had he gotten out of his own clothes, she wondered?

And then she quickly lost interest in the answer as he slid slowly within her and began to move with smooth strokes. She gasped as the warmth became hot, and the hot became a pressure that built and built until she thought she could take no more. Her fingers dug into the hard muscles of his back. She writhed beneath him, demanding some release, demanding something she couldn't even put a name to right now.

The moments seemed to stretch out into forever. Her old life seemed a thousand miles away. Then she cried out as the tautness suddenly overflowed, filling her with a hot flush.

She shuddered, and somewhere inside her a vital seam threatened, then gave.

THEY STAYED IN BED even after the day had begun to close up like a tulip. David had left the room only long enough to leave a note under his grandmother's door, then jumped beneath the covers again.

They must have dozed off, because the bedside clock said it was nearly seven in the evening when Addy woke. She turned her head. Heat rose within her as she realized that David was awake, as well, watching her in the darkness. His hand clicked on the bedside light.

Addy squinted against the brightness, pulling the sheet up to cover her breasts. David reached out to sift a displaced curl back behind her ear. He smiled as he scanned her face, and she instantly knew where his mind was taking him.

"Lord, here's a modern miracle," he said very low. "A woman who can still blush when she has wicked thoughts."

The remark only brought more heat to her cheeks. Ignoring her embarrassment, she said, "How do you know I was having wicked thoughts?"

"Because I'd like to think they mirror

mine." He hugged her closer to his side as she kissed his bare chest. "Are you all right?"

"I'm fine. Better than fine, actually."

He sighed. "I wish we could stay here forever, but you know we can't, of course. The real world awaits. But, God, I wish it didn't."

"For a guy who thinks he's so practical, you're doing a lot of wishing."

He turned on his side and gave her a look that was suddenly serious. "I'll tell you what I really wish, Addy. I wish those ten years had never happened. I wish I could go back and change everything."

She wished that, too. How different things might have been. "You can't," she said on a note of regret. "All we can do is move forward."

She started to rise, but he reached out a hand to stop her. "Why did we ever let those ten years get away from us? I know we said a lot of harsh things to one another, but we should have gotten past that."

"We were very young. At the time it didn't seem possible. And then the years just went by—"

He squeezed her arm, making her glance

back at him. "We shouldn't have allowed it to drift away. Look what it's cost us."

She drew her bottom lip between her teeth. "I'm sorry now that I didn't tell you about the baby. I should have."

There was a tense second of silence. Her fingers fidgeted with the edge of the sheet. One of David's hands moved to cover them, and they remained a willing captive. When she didn't turn to look at him, however, he sat up and brought his other hand to her chin, swinging her head slowly to face him. "It's all right, Addy. What's done is done. But let's not let any more time get away from us. Come with me to Los Angeles."

CHAPTER SIXTEEN

ADDY PULLED BACK TO look at him. He'd sounded calm and unbelievably confident. She made a move to rise. "I should get going."

"Addy, wait a minute. You can't just leave and pretend I didn't say it. I don't want this to be all there is for us."

Pulled to her knees in front of him, she gave him a small smile. She was determined to place a black curtain across her mind, to block out all thought. "David, it's all right." She lifted a finger to his chin, trailing it along his hardened jawline. "What we just shared was wonderful. But it *is* all there is. All there can be. You have your life in Los Angeles. I have mine here. Nothing's changed for us."

Anger flashed in his eyes. Quiet and scorching. "*Everything's* changed for us. I don't want to lose another ten years."

"Why are you making this so difficult? You know my plans."

"A child but no husband?" He shook his head. "I don't understand that. How did you get to that place?"

"I didn't get there. I was *taken* there. By life. I've waited ten years to find someone who could share that dream. I wanted a man I could love, a man who would gladly make babies with me. It just didn't happen. But just because I don't have a husband doesn't mean I can't be happy raising a child of my own."

"You'll make a wonderful mother, Addy. But you're meant for more than that."

"Maybe I am. But in the meantime I can build my own life with a child and a job that pleases me. I'm not going to sit around waiting for it to come to *me* anymore."

"So don't. Move out to Los Angeles. Live with me. Make a life with me there."

She should have seen that coming. Lovers. For however long it lasted. But how could she accept that kind of bargain when what she wanted was a lifetime? A husband. A family. Her heart felt shredded. "You make it sound so easy," she said, wishing he'd turn her loose.

"It *is* easy. I know Hollywood isn't your kind of place—"

"It isn't."

"But there are a dozen places nearby where we could live. I'll commute if I have to."

It was a kind concession for him to make, but eventually it just wouldn't work. For either of them. "David—"

His hands encircled her arms, trying to make her see reason. "Give yourself some time to think things through. Six months. If you're still determined to have a baby all by yourself, then you can do it there. But you don't *have* to make the lodge your life, Addy. You don't have to keep taking a bunch of tinhorn tourists out on camping trips. You're a smart woman. You can do other things."

She shook out of his grasp and rose, the sheet wrapped around her. She felt her own anger rise. They really were worlds apart and they were only going to make it worse if she didn't stop it now.

"You don't get it, do you? Of course I don't *have* to do any of those things. I *want* to do them. I love living out here. I love living close to my family and contributing to the success of the business. This is where I always dreamed of raising a family. There's nothing in Los Angeles for me."

"*I'll* be in Los Angeles. Why can't that be enough for you? At least in the beginning."

In his eyes she read bitterness and regret and the beginnings of a terrible acceptance. The light caught the lines of fatigue etched across his features. Something in his stillness was almost ominous, but she refused to look away from him.

He raked a hand through his hair. "I'll make it work for you, Addy. Whatever it takes, I'll make it work. We didn't have faith in one another ten years ago. Can't you have faith in me now?"

She almost gave it up right there and then. It sounded so possible, and if anyone could do the *im*possible, it was David. But…

She stretched out a hand to caress the side of his face. "I know you'd do everything you could to make it work for us. And for a while it would be enough." She shook her head and dropped her hand. "But by your own admission, you're a workaholic. How long before you began to resent all the concessions you'd have to make to be able to spend time with me? A month? Two?"

"If I'm a workaholic it's because I've never had a good enough reason to spend much time away from the office. But if you're there, I'll begrudge every minute I'm *not* with you."

"Maybe at first. But I can't just be your playmate out there, David. I can't just wait around for you to come home. There has to be something else for me, too. Because sooner or later, I'd resent my life as well. We'd resent each other, and that would spell disaster for both of us. We can't—"

"We can. We can sort this out."

"I have to go," Addy said, searching around for her clothes. "I have a camping trip to prepare for and I'm…" Her voice dried up, dying in the back of her throat.

David stared at her from the bed, his hands dangling over his knees. He looked awful. Wounded from the inside out. "Addy…" he began hoarsely. "If you go now, you won't see me again. I'll be gone when you get back."

She went still, faced with the truth of that statement. Then she walked over to the bed. "I know," she said. She kissed him gently on the lips. He didn't flinch or try to take her into his arms. He was completely still. "Goodbye, David."

IN TWO WEEKS DAVID WAS in San Francisco.

He'd been there many times before, of course. Twice on a shoot and several times for various pitch meetings that had accomplished very little. He knew it was a city full of life, interesting and colorful, though he'd never personally experienced it that way.

Today he and Rob had flown up to attend a party hosted by Lee Carthage. *That* Lee Carthage. A cash cow as far as box office receipts were concerned. The actor had just signed on as the lead in David's production of *The Man Behind the Mask*. It had taken months of negotiating to ink the deal, but it was done now, and Carthage wanted to celebrate the occasion tonight at his beach home. A small affair, he'd promised, and David suspected that meant no more than a couple hundred people.

He hated those kinds of parties. All the backslapping and backstabbing that went on over ridiculously expensive bottles of champagne. The false brilliance, the giddy indiscretions of grown men and women who couldn't control their addictions. The hosts generous and ruthless at the same moment, always on the lookout for opportunity. It made his skin crawl.

But he knew he had to attend. *The Man Behind the Mask* had all the makings of a blockbuster. All the players were onboard now, and frankly even David had to acknowledge it would be foolhardy to piss off one of the biggest names in Hollywood, if not *the* biggest name, by dissing his party. So he'd go and smile and laugh and make small talk, all the while hoping for an early evening.

At least he didn't have to worry about staying at Carthage's place. Claiming he had meetings throughout the day, David had begged off and told his secretary to make the usual arrangements. He wasn't sure what the "usual arrangements" were anymore—things just got done in his office—but now he found himself in a penthouse suite on

Powell Street. All glass and muted colors and sleek lines. Beneath the windows lay the bustling downtown corridors of the city, with Coit Tower in the background and the bay gleaming in diamond sunlight in the distance.

It reminded him of Lightning Lake that last day at the lodge, and whether he wanted to or not, he couldn't help remembering.

All of it.

Those days on the trail to the Devil's Smile. Taking Addy in his arms to share a dance at Clementine's. The insanely sudden dive his stomach had taken when she'd fallen from her horse. The moonlight touching the soft contours of her body as she'd stretched naked against him.

Addy, Addy, Addy.

There were a hundred images in his mind, pieces of memories that just wouldn't go away. He yanked at his thoughts again, as he had so many times in the past two weeks, and forced them to the thing that must be faced.

He had lost her.

And though a sharp pang went through his body with that knowledge, he knew he had to ignore it. The problems between them had been laid out. David knew the why, the how, all of it now. He'd moved past anger to regret, and the bottom line was they were done. Finished. No turning back.

"We have a few hours before the party," Rob said behind him. "What would you like to do? Go over the Blankenship agreement?"

David knew he should say yes. In a month his next picture would be opening nation-wide—*Breakneck*. Strictly a no-brainer action flick, but it ought to do well with the male demographic. There were still advertising and distribution and promotion issues to be settled, and while he'd been playing in Colorado, all that had been limping along.

But though he could force himself to remember that he'd once been challenged by this repetitive minutiae, this tedious, obsessive work that had made him very, very rich, he just couldn't do it. Not right now.

He turned from the window. Rob was a great second-in-command, a go-getter. In a few years he'd know everything about the business. And then what? "Let me ask you something, Rob. Where do you see yourself in five years?"

His assistant frowned a little. The two men had become friends, but David seldom indulged in chitchat, so he wasn't surprised to see that he had caught Rob off guard.

"You mean professionally?" the younger man asked. Then, without waiting for an answer, he added, "I suppose I see myself where you are right now."

"And you think that will make you happy?"

"Sure. Why wouldn't it? The money. The glamour. The power. What's not to love? I mean, you've got it all. The magic touch. I figure if I pay attention, in a few years some of that magic will have rubbed off on me."

David shook his head. "It isn't magic. You're chasing an illusion."

Rob huffed out a short laugh. "Well, let me keep chasing it then. Because one day I intend to be very rich and very powerful."

"It won't make you happier. It will only make you miserable in a better neighborhood. Nothing's worth a thing if you—"

David broke off, disgusted with himself. Aw, hell. He was a fine one to lecture anyone. He felt suddenly bleached with fatigue, and a claustrophobic need to escape overtook him. He snatched up a key card from the coffee table and strode across the room. "I'm going out for a while."

Looking startled and unsure of himself, Rob made a move toward the telephone. "Shall I have the car brought around?"

"No," David said quickly. "I need the fresh air."

"David, if I said anything—"

"You didn't. I just need to walk."

He left the room before Rob could say any more.

He spent the rest of the morning and most of the afternoon seeing the sights like a regular tourist. The seals at Pier 39. Chinatown. Fisherman's Wharf. Even Alcatraz. The city was a cultural puzzle, full of energy and charm, with a scent in the air you could almost taste.

Somewhere along the way he came across a cluttered electronics shop selling the latest gadgets and got it in his head that he might send his grandmother a new camcorder. He bought a sleek, light contraption with more buttons and lights than the cockpit of a 747.

Almost immediately after walking out of the shop he worried that it would be too complicated for Gran to operate, but instead of taking it back, he made the decision to test it out himself.

Within five minutes he was filming the cable cars and doing a voice-over explanation for his grandmother's sake. With camera in hand, he began to shed his bad mood like a skin. It felt good to create film again, and some of the old techniques came back to him. Gran would love this silly video, and maybe he could convince her to meet him here soon so they could play tourist together.

Time passed and the sun began to set over the water. When David glanced at his watch, he was surprised to discover it was already past six. Where had the day gone? He was going to be late for the party.

He called Rob and told him to head over to Carthage's place without him, that he'd be there as soon as he could. The man took that news fairly well, though David could tell he was thrown by the idea that his boss could ever be late for anything, including a social obligation.

Well, there was a first time for everything, wasn't there?

HE ENDED UP ARRIVING an hour late and didn't feel a bit repentant. Lee Carthage's house, perched on the cliff overlooking the Pacific, was filled to overflowing and just exactly what David had expected—big and pretentious.

He scanned the crowd and saw what he always found at these kinds of affairs. A sideshow of beautiful people. The wealthy, the corrupt, the aggressively street-smart and desperate climbers. Within twenty minutes he was looking at his watch, longing for the peace and quiet of the penthouse suite.

"David!" Someone tugged hard on David's arm, and he found himself face-to-face with Lee Carthage. Rob was right behind him. "Rob said you were on your way, but I was beginning to give up hope. Grab yourself a drink, man. I want to run something by you."

Even if David hadn't instinctively guessed that Lee was half-drunk, it was obvious by the raised eyebrow and eye contact that Rob laid on him.

Trouble with the talent, that look said, and David felt his chest tighten.

Although Lee Carthage had a gift for making every female his slave and every male his buddy, he was known to become overbearing once he'd had too much to drink.

The music and laughter around them made conversation almost impossible, but Carthage seemed determined. He scooped a flute of champagne off a passing waiter's tray, handed it to David and swept him into the closest alcove. Rob, always ready to lend a hand, came, too.

Lee Carthage shook his head wildly. "I am *so* psyched about this film, man. It's a dream role. We are going to make buckets. You realize that, don't you?"

David took a slow sip of champagne. "I'm certainly hoping that's the case," he said, though it occurred to him in that moment that lately he'd thought very little about what kind of money this film would pull down.

"I've been reading and rereading the script. And I've been thinking…."

Uh-oh, here it comes, David thought. He knew what Carthage could bring to *The Man*

Behind the Mask, but it was never a good thing when the guy spent too much time thinking. He just wasn't good at it.

"My part," Carthage said, pursing his lips. They were wet and too full. David tried not to focus on them. "I think my part needs a little...tweaking."

"Tweaking?"

"My character. He's supposed to have a real ax to grind against the French, right? They killed his family. Stole his land. Who wouldn't be ready to whip up on someone's ass for that? But in those scenes when he's in the Bastille...he's coming off as too much of a wuss. My fans don't want to see tears from Lee Carthage. What are they going to say if I play it that way?"

"I hope they'll say you're a fine actor."

"You know what I mean."

"What do you want?" David asked carefully.

"I want to be comfortable with who the man behind the mask really is. I want to *wear* him like a second skin."

Not tonight, David thought. *I don't have the patience for this crap tonight.*

He downed the champagne in one swallow and set the flute on a nearby table. "So sleep with the script. You have two months. You can know him inside and out by then."

Carthage grinned as though David had been joking. Which he had not. "I guess I just need to say it flat out. I want to rewrite those scenes. Maybe a few others."

David tried not to overreact. He remembered a time not long ago when this kind of demand wouldn't have fazed him in the least. Just part of the business. Half the actors in Hollywood thought they were creative geniuses. But, oh, he was *so* not in the mood for this.

He shook his head slowly. "No. Not possible."

"Of course it's possible," Carthage said. "I rewrote half the pages in *Winning Streak* for Nederland. I know what my public expects from me. I can bring home the bacon on this baby, but it has to be done my way. I want script approval."

"Too late. You just signed a contract, Lee. And nowhere in it was there a mention of script approval."

Carthage didn't look worried. He was a

man used to getting his own way. Behind him Rob's eyes had begun to widen. "The producers and directors I work with understand that I need to be kept happy. *This* will make me happy." He blew air noisily through his nose. "Come on, man. This script was written by an under-the-radar hack who was waiting tables six months ago. He won't mind."

"But I will."

Carthage scrubbed a hand over his face, mussing those famous good looks as he began to lose his temper. "This is not the way to start a picture, McKay. You realize who I am. What I bring to the table. Do you really want to screw with me?"

David had had enough. "Read your contract, glamour boy. Your ass is mine for the duration of this picture. You'll honor your contract with me and with the audience that loves that book and wants to see it done right. You'll hit your marks and say your lines just the way the director tells you to. Or you'll find yourself tied up in court so long that by the time you bust loose they won't want you for a dog food commercial." He tilted his head and smiled thinly at Carthage as the actor stared openmouthed. "You understand?"

Many moments passed while the two men just glared at one another. Rob looked back and forth between them, and David suspected that, for the first time in many years, his assistant was at a complete loss for words.

There was a flurry of red sequins as a beautiful blonde latched onto Lee Carthage's arm. The latest girlfriend. "Lee, honey!" she said sweetly. "No more shop talk. Come dance with me."

Carthage didn't move right away, but it was finally sinking in. He wasn't going to win this battle. He seemed to understand that he'd picked the wrong time, the wrong topic, the wrong person. People were turning, beginning to stare. With one final look of anger tinted with confusion, Carthage whirled and was absorbed into the crowd immediately.

Neither David nor Rob said a word for a long time. A waiter flitted past, and David reached out with both hands, snatching up two huge shrimp on skewers. He handed one to Rob.

"Might as well eat," he ordered. He motioned toward the crowd, who were getting drunker by the moment. "It's not much to show for four billion years of evolution, is it?"

"I don't know what…" Rob began. "What just happened?"

"You mean with Carthage?" David asked, pretending he didn't have a clue. "Was I too rough?"

Rob still looked stunned. "You're one of the best producers in Hollywood. A genius who knows what to leave alone and what to take out. You stay focused in the face of pressure and you've always bred a feeling of security on a set. But what you just did…"

"I know." David turned his head and grinned at his assistant. "I guess I'm not myself lately."

Rob laughed nervously. "I think you have that right. So what now? Should I start damage control?"

David fixed him with a hard stare. "Rob, you do that and you can brush up your résumé." He popped the last of the shrimp into his mouth and ditched the skewer. He felt detached and strangely calm, as though he'd barely awakened from a sound sleep. Time to go. "Stay as long as you like," he said. "I'm going back to the suite."

He did just that. Standing on the penthouse balcony, David watched the night deepen, watched the lights of the city gradually blink out. Rob came in around one in the morning but had the good sense to go straight to his own bedroom.

David stayed where he was. Breathing in the sweet night air. Just breathing.

Knowing that a door that had been opened for him less than a month ago in the Colorado mountains could not be closed again.

CHAPTER SEVENTEEN

IN THE MONTH SINCE David had gone back to Los Angeles, Addy had tried. She really had.

She had immersed herself in hard work. There were always a million things to do at the lodge, and she eagerly threw herself into doing them.

She'd talked her brothers into helping her expand the corral behind the stable. Reining in her patience, she'd taught her father how to create financial spreadsheets on his computer. She'd designed a new brochure for the lodge, then distributed it personally to all the local businesses where Lightning River advertised. She'd dusted and scrubbed and cooked until her hands were raw. It didn't matter what was asked of her. She did it because every early day and long night brought her to a state of exhaustion and gave her what she wanted more than anything else in the world—dreamless sleep.

It was, perhaps, not the most mature way to handle losing the man she loved. The man, she acknowledged now, she had never stopped loving. But it was a start. It deadened the pain of thinking of David.

Sooner or later that pain would fade as it had before. In its place would be the lingering ache of loss. Hard and cold and permanent. But she would learn to deal with it. She had to.

She wished that things were moving faster on the baby front.

She'd gone down to Denver to take care of the paperwork, to run through a dozen tests that would determine if she could and should seek this solution. She'd viewed donor catalogs, waded through baby pictures and even been assigned her own Donor Matching Consultant. It had all been handled very professionally, very tastefully. She felt ready to get on with it.

But oddly enough, the real delay seemed to be within herself. She couldn't seem to make a decision just which donor could be her child's father. It was maddening to be so indecisive, to have her thoughts so muddled. But she'd get better at it. A decision *would* be made.

Because the thought of never feeling any better than she did right now was unendurable.

Addy settled back on her haunches, wiping the edge of her hand over her brow. Though fall would soon arrive and the mountains would turn into a patchwork quilt of green pines and yellow aspens, it was still warm here on the back porch of the lodge. She'd been working for hours, replanting some of her mother's herbs into bigger pots. The air was fresh with the scents of rosemary, thyme and oregano.

Her neck ached. She rotated her shoulders a few times, trying to work out the kinks. Behind her the door opened and closed, and she glanced back to see Rafe coming to join her.

She looked up at him, offering a broad, totally false smile she'd become master of lately. He pulled up one of the wooden benches, straddled it and watched her work for a few minutes.

Finally he said, "It won't make any difference, you know."

"What won't?"

"Doing all this extra work around here. Pop's not going to bump you up in his will. You'll always have to share with Nick, Matt and me."

This time Addy's smile was genuine. "I guess I'll just have to settle for whatever I can get then."

Rafe's eyebrow quirked. "You never used to *settle* for anything. That's why you were always my favorite sister."

"Not to mention your *only* sister. But I was younger then. I thought anything was possible."

"So now you're old and used up and nothing is possible?"

"So now I'm all *grown* up and very, very wise," she said.

Her brother laughed. He reached out to flick his finger across her nose. "You have a smudge of dirt on your nose, oh, wise one."

She reached for the clean rag in her back pocket and scrubbed it across her face. When Rafe nodded that she'd gotten the spot, she went back to work, pressing moist potting soil around the base of a container of leafy parsley.

He watched her as if fascinated, though she suspected he wasn't. "So how long has it been?" he asked at last.

"How long has it been since what?"

"Since David left."

The question caught Addy off guard, and she took a quick breath. She'd forgotten how, of all her brothers, Rafe was the one who could read people like human Rorschach tests.

"I don't know," she said, forcing the words past the lump in her chest. "A month maybe." She heard herself add silently...*and four days*... Oh, how pathetic she was.

Disgusted with herself, she shook her head sharply and met Rafe's eyes. "Don't look at me like that. I'm over him."

"So you say," Rafe responded in a skeptical tone. "Certainly the family makes the effort to appear like we believe that."

Pride blazed within her. She gave him a censuring look. "Help me with these pots or go away and leave me alone. I have work to do."

He paid no attention to that. He touched her back, a gesture of compassion and pity. She flinched away from it, and he didn't try again. Instead he said, "Addy, listen to me. You can work yourself into the grave, but it's not going to solve anything. If you're really in love with the guy, why are you here while he's in Los Angeles? Why couldn't you give it a shot?"

She'd asked herself that very question a number of times. But because she always ended up with the same answer, she fired a furious glare at her brother. "Since when did you become the love doctor?"

"I'm like a reformed alcoholic. Since I fell in love with Dani and found out how wonderful life could be with the right person, I want everyone to feel this good. It's like a sweet grape on your tongue, Addy. You can almost taste the happiness."

Her anger dissipated as she gaped at him. How different Rafe was from the man who had come home last Christmas. "I wish you could see your face right now," she said gently.

He ducked his head, smiling but obviously a little embarrassed. When he looked at her again, he said softly, "I can't help it. Dani's pregnant."

Addy gasped. "That's wonderful!" She wiped her hands quickly on the rag and leaned over to hug him. "I'm so glad for you."

"Thanks." They hugged again. When they separated at last with a little self-conscious laugh, Rafe caught Addy's chin between his fingers. He sobered and gave her an earnest look. "Everything's going to work out for you, too, Ad. With this baby thing. And David. You'll see."

She wanted to believe that, but it seemed too foolish to hope. But she knew Rafe meant well, and really, she didn't want to think about David any more right now. It was just too hard.

As she gave her brother a noncommittal smile, he said, "Why don't you come out with us tonight? Everyone's going to dinner and a movie. Even Mom and Pop. We haven't had a family night out in a long time."

She made a face. "I don't know…I wanted to—"

"What? Clean out your closet? Alphabetize Mom's spices? Hang new curtains? Come on. Stop trying to forget old what's-his-name and spend some time with the people who really love you. This is your home, Ad. It can't be haunted by someone who hasn't got the sense to see that my baby sister is just about the best woman in the world for him."

A few hours' reprieve from the misery of missing David. That would be heavenly. She made the decision quickly, before she could change her mind. "Okay. You've convinced me. What time?"

"Six-thirty. We'll go to the movie, then hit Golden Pagoda for Chinese."

"Great! What movie?"

"*Breakneck*. At the Majestic."

"Oh…"

"I know. You like something a little more cerebral. But that's our only choice unless we go down to Idaho Springs."

"No, it's not that. It's just…" *Breakneck* was the new movie by David's company, McKay Worldwide. It was silly to mind, but she couldn't help the reflexive response.

"Oh, hell," Rafe grumbled. "I just

realized. That's lover boy's latest movie, isn't it? But listen, it's not like he's the star. You'll see his name on the credits, but that's all. Surely you can deal with that much?"

"Of course I can," she said brightly. "In fact, I'm looking forward to it."

THE MAJESTIC WAS THE only theater in Broken Yoke. It was closed on Mondays and Tuesdays. The rest of the week it held two showings a night of the latest Hollywood had to offer. Because it was small, without plush seating or even cup holders, movie buffs in search of an enjoyable viewing experience often bypassed it for the megaplex down in Idaho Springs.

Addy hadn't been to a movie in ages and she didn't want to be at the cinema now. But how could she have refused without looking completely hopeless?

The theater was full of family members, plus a few other people she knew. Rafe led her to the center of an aisle. She felt like a fifth wheel, with him and Dani on one side and Matt and Leslie on the other. Mom and Pop sat directly in front, with Nick and Kari beside them. Tonight Nick's daughter Tessa was babysitting their little boy and Rafe's young daughter, Frannie.

Rafe was right. This should be a fun evening out. Even if the movie proved to be a dud, it was nice to have most of the family all together. She must stop wishing she was home.

Just as everyone settled in Addy saw Geneva McKay and Polly Swinburne slip into seats a couple of rows in front of her. She hadn't seen Geneva much since David's departure. A couple of times on the street. Once in the grocery. When they'd run into one another, Geneva had seemed uncomfortable and she never mentioned David.

The old woman caught sight of the D'Angelos. She waved and sat down quickly next to Polly as the lights went down. Addy couldn't imagine that *Breakneck* would be the kind of movie Geneva would like. She was probably just interested in anything that had David's name attached to it.

The previews started. Nothing remotely interesting to Addy. She moved her feet, restless, knowing it was too late now to get up and leave.

The movie began. She watched the logo flash across the screen. *A McKay Worldwide Production.* Only a flicker of discomfort in the pit of her stomach. Not too bad.

In a few minutes she'd see David's name as the producer. Her heart felt erratic. *It's just his name. You can do this, Addy.*

Rafe's hand moved to squeeze hers in the darkness. He leaned close. "You all right?"

"Yes," she whispered.

She got through it.

Somehow she managed to shut out all thought, all memory, and become absorbed in the story. *Breakneck* was no Oscar contender, a pretty basic plot about a man trying to clear his name after being framed for murder. The guys in the audience seemed to like the action. The women—including Addy—didn't mind having the latest Hollywood hottie to look at, and at least there was *some* character development in the love story. All around her the crowd seemed to be enjoying it. So should she.

And then, in the last few minutes of the film, after everyone had been brought to justice and the movie began to wind down, Addy found her most difficult moment.

The hero of the movie, Jason, lay in a hospital bed, bruised and bloody. Then the heroine, Rebecca, rushed into the room and flew to his side. She wasn't a bad little actress, managing to convey both hope and regret on a face that had probably paid half a dozen visits to a cosmetic surgeon.

She took Jason's hand, drawing it to her collagen-injected lips. "Can you ever forgive me?" she begged in a ragged voice. "I should have trusted you. You're the best thing that's ever happened to me, and I almost lost you. Tell me it's not too late for us."

Addy grimaced. Of course it wasn't too late. That was the difference between the movies and reality. You got second chances. You could demolish your life single-handedly and still get the guy. Nine times out of ten, happy endings for everyone. Oh, she really ought to stop going to the movies. They were a complete waste of time and so unrealistic.

And that's when it hit her out of the blue. Just like that. No warning, no deep thinking and absolutely no possibility of misunderstanding.

If the dream of making a life with David

had wilted in her hands, whose fault was that, really? He had wanted to give them another chance. He had wanted to make up for all those lost years. He'd asked her to give it six months. But foolishly she'd been unwilling to try it his way. Fear. Stubborn pride. Just look where that had gotten her. Too late she understood that this was a love she should have fought for.

Rebecca and Jason reunited. Addy sat in the dark, remaining motionless. She simply stared at the screen, even when the credits began to roll.

There was such pain in losing David, but it was far worse to have lost him and realize that she had only herself to blame.

But was it really too late to do anything about it? Was there any way, any way at all, that she could salvage something?

The lights went up and she blinked. She sat still, waiting for the small crowd to clear out.

Rafe nudged her shoulder. "Well, what did you think?"

She wanted to seem unfazed, maybe even a little blasé. There was no need for anyone in the family to know that her mind was racing a mile a minute, trying on ideas and rejecting them one after the other. They would think she was certifiable.

"It was all right," she replied with a shrug. "I guess anything resembling a believable plot would have been too much to ask. What was the director's theory, I wonder? If we can't convince them, let's confuse them?"

Someone laughed and said, "Everyone's a movie critic."

David.

Her head whipped around to find him sitting directly behind her. He was here, and she knew in that instant that he had been in the theater all along.

Maybe someday she'd wish she had handled it a little better. But the truth was, in that moment she couldn't. She was so deliriously happy to see him that she was beyond responding in any remotely sensible way.

Consumed, engulfed with wanting, Addy stood so quickly that her seat slapped back into place with a bang. She felt her heart tumble and crash as she stepped over the seat and toppled into David's aisle. Into his arms.

"You're here," she gasped out and planted a kiss against his mouth. "You're really here."

"In the flesh," he said. He held her in a life-saving grip, laughing a little at her enthusiasm. "Can I take this as a sign that you're glad to see me?"

"You have no idea." Filled with amazement and hope that, against all odds, a second chance had been given to her, Addy anchored her gaze on the top button of his shirt, determined to tell him everything. "I'm so sorry, David. I've been so stupid, thinking I don't need you in my life. But I do. I can't help it." She looked up into his eyes, her throat so dry it hurt to swallow. "Like Rebecca said to Jason, 'Tell me it's not too late for us.'"

His eyes glowed with a mischievous light. "You do realize that I'm *not* nearly as good-looking as Jason, don't you?"

She lifted her eyes to his. "I don't want Jason. I want you. I love you."

Someone close by cleared their throat, and Addy jerked around to see Rafe grinning at her. The rest of the D'Angelo clan was standing in the aisles. They were all smiling at her, too.

She frowned at Rafe. "You tricked me."

He nodded. "I did. I was told to get you here. And I'm pleased to see that my old talents haven't deserted me."

"Speaking of deserting..." her mother spoke up. "I think it's time we all left these two alone to talk."

"Not yet!" Sam protested.

"Right *now*, Sam," Rose said simply, and Sam filed out of the aisle without another peep.

Geneva and Polly had moved into the aisle now, too. David's grandmother slipped past the seats to hug them both. She touched her grandson's cheek. "It's all up to you now, dear."

From nearby Polly said, "Just don't mess it up, Hollywood."

In a few minutes everyone had left. The theater was empty. She had no idea how David had managed it, but not even the usher came in to clean.

She turned in David's arms. "Don't mess up what?"

"What I've come here to say."

"David—"

He placed a finger over her lips. "Uh-uh.

Last time we were together, you did most of the talking. Now it's my turn. I came all this way to get things straight between us, and now I'm going to."

The firm tone of his voice startled her into silence.

"That's better." He glanced around. "Is it just me or does this theater need renovation?"

She punched his arm. "David, please don't torture me. Isn't it enough that I've embarrassed myself in front of my family and confessed that I love you?"

"No. Say it again."

"I love you. I always have and I always will. I don't care what I have to do to make it work. I'll go to Los Angeles. I'll get a job. Just as long as we can be together."

"That won't work. I don't want you to come to Los Angeles."

"You don't?" A shiver crept along her nerves. "Why not?"

"Because I'll be here, so having you there will be rather inconvenient."

"What?" Addy shook her head. "What are you talking about?"

"*Breakneck* is my last movie as head of McKay Worldwide. I sold it. I'm officially out of the film-producing business. I hope it does well, because the money will have to keep coming from somewhere for a while. How much does a house in Broken Yoke go for these days?"

She stared at him as he brushed his thumb over the hollow of her cheek. "So you're just going to retire?"

"Of course not. I have plenty of ideas. I thought it was time to see if I still had that fire in my belly to do documentaries."

Shocked, Addy pulled back slightly from his embrace. "Are you serious?"

"I certainly hope so. I've spent the last month rearranging things so it can happen. So what do you think? I figure I'll have to go off on research trips sometimes, but you could come with me and tote my camera. Around your work at the stable, of course. Are you interested?"

"Yes." The word came out so easily that she said it again, this time against his mouth as it closed over hers in a sensual kiss.

Eventually his lips tickled against the shell

of her ear, and the soft feather of his breath warmed her skin. "You realize that I'll be the trail boss this time. You have to do what *I* say."

"I will. But could you at least make me your assistant?"

"I've got a better idea. Why don't I officially make you my wife? It will make things a lot easier if you agree to marry me as soon as possible."

Stunned, she could do nothing more than look at him for a long minute. His eyes were brimming with excitement and his tremulous smile pierced her heart.

"Say something," he said at last.

"I can't. I'm…"

"Adriana D'Angelo, speechless at last. That doesn't happen every day." When she continued to say nothing, he added, "We wasted ten years, Addy, and I'll always regret that. But we aren't going to waste ten more. Not even ten minutes. I want you to marry me."

"You realize that I still want children."

"Fine. Anything wrong with having mine?"

"Not a thing."

"Then let's do it the old-fashioned way. Let's make a baby, Addy."

He cupped her face in his hands and kissed her again. Long and deeply. A kiss tinged with passion and promise. The ripples of her happiness widened and widened. She sighed against him. It was an almost unbearable relief to be in his arms again.

"I've been so miserable since you left," she admitted.

"I know."

She lifted her head. "How?"

"Your family told me. And Gran. I had to let them know what I had planned pretty quickly in case you decided to get over me by getting pregnant or interested in someone else."

"Someone else? Impossible."

Pressed against his chest, she heard his rumbling chuckle. "I was counting on that."

"You're very sure of yourself."

"I am now. He brought his fingers to her chin, lifting her head so their eyes met. "For so long I've been a guest in my own life, Addy. But when I came back here, when I was with you again, I felt like the years just melted away. I want someone who will believe in me the way you did—the way you do. I love you so much and I want to spend the rest of my life making you glad that you're my wife."

Pleasure moved through her in waves. She snuggled against David again, her hip bone pressed against his, her arms wrapped around his chest so tightly that she thought she could feel every rib. They stood like that a long time, touching, kissing. She felt the smooth passage of his hand over her hair, followed by the warmth of his lips.

Over the hot pulse of desire that rushed through her, Addy heard a noise in the aisle and turned her head. Pop had come back into the theater.

"Come on, you two," he said. "You can spend the rest of your life canoodling. Right now we want to celebrate. We're all hungry and we want Chinese."

Giving them both a look of complete understanding, he turned and marched back up the aisle.

"We don't have to go," Addy said.

David grinned at her. "Of course we have to.

After all they went through to get us back together, do you really think your father and my grandmother are going to let us sneak away?"

"Not likely."

"Besides, if I'm going to be part of a big Italian family, I might as well start figuring out how that works right now."

David took her hand in his and led her out into the aisle. Anchored against his side, her heart nearly bursting with love, they went out to join the family.

EPILOGUE

IT WAS SUMMER AGAIN before everything seemed to fall into place. Nearly a year had passed since that night in the theater, and sometimes Addy thought it had gone by in the blink of an eye.

A year of high points and major changes—a wedding, a move into a house in Broken Yoke. Lifestyle adjustments and small concessions. Learning each other's likes and dislikes as if they were new lovers, which in some ways they were. Sometimes it was a challenge. Sometimes there were long nights spent making love under the stars. But minute by minute, day by day, they had found their way.

"Believe it or not, I'm nervous," David said as he slid up behind Addy, placing his hands around her waist.

He had pulled her into the lodge's library to steal a kiss before they joined everyone in the dining room.

"There's no need to be," she replied, turning into his embrace. "It's wonderful."

"Your family is a notoriously tough crowd."

"If anyone throws tomatoes, they'll have to deal with me."

David let his hand drift across Addy's belly. It was flat, but in a few months it wouldn't be. The doctor had confirmed that only last week. It hadn't really been a shock. They'd been trying for months to make it happen.

"Hiding behind a pregnant woman," David said. "What will people think?"

"They'll think I must love you very much. And they'd be right."

She relaxed against him, letting her hands explore dangerous territory. She wished they could slip away and go out to the lake, where the cool July breeze could caress their skin while they caressed one another. Around David, sometimes it was so hard to keep from behaving like a horny teenager.

But not tonight, she thought. At least…not for a while.

Tonight Pop had closed down the dining room for a private family party. After catering hundreds of birthdays and wedding receptions, it was the first time the lodge had ever hosted something like this. A postpremiere party for David's first documentary film.

After months of hard work, *In Their Memory* was officially in the can.

Using his grandmother's trip out to the Devil's Smile as inspiration, David had decided on a film about the different ways a family chose to honor their loved ones who'd passed on. With Addy's help, he had tracked down so many families, all of them intent on keeping memories alive one way or another.

A man who'd had his late wife's face tattooed all over his body. The family that had single-handedly built a town library in honor of their book-loving mother. Two women in Alabama who had lost their fathers in wars, and who now owned a cottage industry of personalized teddy bears fashioned out of old uniforms of soldiers who had never been forgotten.

Addy couldn't imagine how it could all come together, but in the end it had paid off. When Addy had watched the footage, she'd found it thought-provoking, sad, mysterious, touching, even funny at times.

And now it was ready. How could an audience not respond to such a universal theme as loss and renewal? she had told David.

He was skeptical enough to remind her that in the film industry nothing was certain. But she could tell he was proud of it, and in a show of determined confidence, he was taking *In Their Memory* to a film festival in August. Addy, of course, would be right by his side.

But first he had wanted to preview it for friends and family. They rented the Majestic, called everyone they cared about and sent them off to see it. Now everyone had returned to the lodge afterward for wine, dessert and conversation.

As Addy walked with David into the packed dining room, she squeezed his hand, trying to convey faith and confidence. If he really *was* nervous, his broad smile didn't give it away.

As soon as they were spotted, there was a warm round of applause. Almost immediately they were surrounded by family members and friends. The consensus was overwhelmingly positive.

It was David's moment, and she let him have it. Last week, when they had announced to the family that she was going to have a baby, he had stepped back and let them overwhelm her with love.

But now it was his turn.

She was so proud of what he had accomplished. She stood beside him, listening to praise and support as so many people came up to congratulate him. Even Polly Swinburne, notoriously stingy with compliments, said that he certainly seemed to have a way with the camera.

David's grandmother and Addy's own parents came up to them together. Geneva looked misty-eyed as she hugged her grandson.

"Oh, David. It was so wonderful," she said on a soft breath of sound. "Your grandfather would be so proud."

"Thank you for saying that, Gran. I

thought about him a lot when I was putting this together."

Standing close, Addy thought she could sense David relaxing a little. He had a lot of confidence about so many things, but she'd known how important it was to him to make this film shine.

Sam, never shy, threw his hands up in the air as though cheering on his favorite football team. *"Fantastico!"* He gave David a narrowed look. "Are you sure you're not Italian? You have an eye for what touches the human heart."

The conversation took off after that. So many questions about how the film had been put together. What film festivals it would be eligible for. How it could be marketed.

In a moment when Sam was explaining to Geneva what part he liked best, David leaned close to Addy. In a hushed voice that was thick and love-filled, he whispered, "I couldn't have done it without you. You know that, don't you? I know how to make a commercially successful film. But your input is what gave it heart."

His lips grazed her cheek. Smiling, Addy

lowered her head, wishing they could leave right now.

Pop never missed a thing. He nudged her mother. "You see, Rosa? Geneva and I were right to get these two back together. We have a talent for this sort of thing."

Rose shook her head. "You have a talent for something. I'm just not sure what it is."

Pop wrapped his arm around her and pulled her close. "I will show you tonight, *cara*."

"Behave, Sam," her mother told him, but Addy could tell that it was only a half-hearted objection.

Dani came up to join them, linked arm in arm with Rafe. Addy greeted them both enthusiastically. She hadn't seen much of them since their baby, a cute little boy they'd named Anthony, had been born a couple months ago.

They chatted awhile, then Dani asked David, "So what's your next project?"

David gave Addy a quick look of affection before answering. "I think I'm going to be busy working with my assistant for a while. The new nursery needs to be painted. I have furniture to put together. I never knew babies needed so many things."

"Neither did I," Rafe said with a laugh. "No more days of traveling light. But you get used to it."

"I tried to tell you." Sam threw in his two cents. "Wait until you have a houseful. It will seem like Grand Central Station."

Addy couldn't help glancing at David to see how he handled that remark. For a long time she'd been nervous about how he would react to the news that she was pregnant. He'd told her from the beginning that he was delighted, and certainly he seemed to be just as excited as she was, sharing every moment. But still…it was a huge change.

"We have a little while yet," she said to him. "Before I get too big, I was thinking we could go out to our place. Just the two of us one last time before the baby comes. That's possible, isn't it?"

Since David had come back to Broken Yoke, they'd discovered just how much they enjoyed exploring the backcountry together. And just as Geneva and Herbert had made the Devil's Smile their own, she and David had a special fondness for the cave where they'd hidden away the scratchings on the wall from prying eyes.

"If you feel up to it," David replied. "Do I get to be trail boss?"

"Trail boss, nursemaid, masseur, manservant—" she winked at him "—anything you want, as long as we get to be there together."

"No mules this time. I hate mules."

"No mules."

"And we'll take more ice."

"Your grandmother is right. You really are high-maintenance."

"Maybe I'll take my laptop," David said, refusing to be sidetracked. "I want to start laying out my next project."

Addy seriously doubted that he'd get much work done out at the cave, but with so many family members around them right now, she didn't want to point that out. And then with a secret smile she thought Mom and Pop and the rest of them probably already knew that they weren't making those trips out to the backcountry just to enjoy the scenery.

After a while, Addy left David talking to

Matt so she and Leslie could check out the dessert table. They caught Frannie, Rafe's eight-year-old daughter, with a plate piled high with cannolis and tiramisu. She looked extremely guilty and would have made a quick getaway if Addy hadn't stopped her with one hand on the back of her blouse.

She turned the girl around, smiling down at her with a censuring look. "Does your mother know you're over here raiding the desserts?" Addy asked.

The girl nodded. "She's the one who sent me. They're for her."

Before Addy could say any more, Frannie slipped away, heading for Dani, who was standing near the door, talking to Sheriff Bendix.

"Do you think that's true?" Leslie asked.

"Could be," Addy said as she lifted a piece of cheesecake off the table. "Dani did gain a bit of weight when she was pregnant, and she said she really misses being able to eat for two." She made a pleased sound as she took a bite of her mother's raspberry and white chocolate cheesecake. "I have to admit, when I eat Mom's desserts, I don't care if I get so big that the elephants throw peanuts back at me if we go to the zoo."

They laughed together, split a cannoli and talked a few minutes about Addy's latest appointment with the obstetrician. It was wonderful to have Leslie in the family. As a nurse, she was such a good person to have around, but as a sister-in-law, she was a great friend.

Matt joined them at the table. As usual, he went for his favorite, the custard-filled pastries. The last time Addy had seen David, he'd been with Matt, but, glancing around quickly, she didn't see her husband anywhere in the room.

"I thought you were with David," she said.

"I was. But now he's in the library with Paranoid Polly."

"With Polly!" Addy exclaimed. She punched her brother lightly on the arm. "You left him alone with Polly? What kind of brother are you?"

"The smart kind. It was every man for himself."

"What do you think they're talking about?"

Locally, Polly Swinburne was famous for

her conspiracy theories. She had dozens of them, everything from milk in Florida cows tainted by the Cubans, to weather machines invented by the Dutch for the sole purpose of driving their European neighbors crazy.

Matt barely looked up from his plate. "I'm betting it's the story."

"What story?"

"You know. The one about how her great, great grandfather and his family were murdered by a nasty group of early settlers in Broken Yoke. Some of *our* forefathers. Hasn't she always said it would make a great movie? I'm betting she's doing the pitch to David right now."

"Oh, no," Addy said. She chewed her bottom lip. "Do you think I should go rescue him?"

"Why? He's a big boy. He can take care of himself. Besides, he knows what Polly's like. He knew all about her when he lived here before."

"But she's so much worse now."

Matt and Leslie laughed together. "Tell us about it," Leslie said. "She shows up at the clinic about once a month with some new rash or mysterious illness that only Matt can cure."

"Maybe I should barge into the library. Pretend that I can't live without him by my side."

Arms suddenly came around Addy's waist and she turned to find David there, grinning down at her. "*Pretend* that you can't live without me?" he scolded. "I guess the honeymoon is finally over."

Addy laughed and hugged him close. Then she gave him such a deep, thorough kiss that his eyes widened a little. When she pulled back, she was nearly out of breath. "Think so?"

"Maybe not," David admitted, and ran an affectionate hand down her cheek. "You were worried about me?"

"Frantic. So…what did Polly want?"

"Why did the founders of Broken Yoke want to murder her family?"

"If they were all like Polly, wouldn't you?" Matt asked.

They chatted for a while, and David told them that he'd agreed to read over the three boxes of undeniable proof Polly had collected showing that her ancestors had been singled out for murder so many years ago.

"Unfortunately," David said, "I told her that it wasn't something I felt I could do justice to. But I'll call Rob. He owes me a favor. She'll get a reading, at least. And who knows, maybe there's some truth in the old girl's story."

"So what are you going to work on next?" Leslie asked.

"It will be a big project. Not too much travel but hours and hours of research. Luckily I have plenty of resources close by that I can draw on."

Addy looked at him in surprise. He hadn't said a word about the next project.

With an amused look on his face, David spread his hands out as though he could already see the marquee. "I'm thinking of calling it *Inside the Italian Family*. What do you think?"

Everyone laughed at that and Matt spoke up. "I think you'll have another winner on your hands. And there's so much we can share with you."

"You already have," David said. He looked at Addy, his eyes full of love. "How about it? Want to help me figure out what everyone needs to know about being part of a big family like the D'Angelos?"

Addy pulled him close for another kiss. "There's only one thing they need to know," she said. "Being a D'Angelo means being loved."

* * * * *

Set in darkness beyond the ordinary world.
Passionate tales of life and death.
With characters' lives ruled by laws the everyday
world can't begin to imagine.

Introducing NOCTURNE, a spine-tingling
new line from Silhouette Books.

The thrills and chills begin with UNFORGIVEN
by Lindsay McKenna

Plucked from the depths of hell, former military sharpshooter Reno Manchahi was hired by the government to kill a thief, but he had a mission of his own. Descended from a family of shape-shifters, Reno vowed to get the revenge he'd thirsted for all these years. But his mission went awry when his target turned out to be a powerful seductress, Magdalena Calen Hernandez, who risked everything to battle a potent evil. Suddenly, Reno had to transform himself into a true hero and fight the enemy that threatened them all. He had to become a Warrior for the Light....

Turn the page for a sneak preview of
UNFORGIVEN by Lindsay McKenna.
On sale September 26,
wherever books are sold.

Chapter 1

One shot...one kill.

The sixteen-pound sledgehammer came down with such fierce power that the granite boulder shattered instantly. A spray of glittering mica exploded into the air and sparkled momentarily around the man who wielded the tool as if it were a weapon. Sweat ran in rivulets down Reno Manchahi's drawn, intense face. Naked from the waist up, the hot July sun beating down on his back, he hefted the sledgehammer skyward once more. Muscles in his thick forearms leaped and biceps bulged. Even his breath was focused on the boulder. In his mind's eye, he pictured Army General Robert Hampton's fleshy, arrogant fifty-year-old features on the rock's surface. Air exploded from between his lips as he brought the avenging hammer down. The boulder pulverized beneath his funneled hatred.

One shot...one kill...

Nostrils flaring, he inhaled the dank, humid heat and drew it deep into his massive lungs. Revenge allowed Reno to endure his imprisonment at a U.S. Navy brig near San Diego, California. Drops of sweat were flung in all directions as the crack of his sledgehammer claimed a third stone victim. Mouth taut, Reno moved to the next boulder.

The other prisoners in the stone yard gave him a wide berth. They always did. They instinctively felt his simmering hatred, the palpable revenge in his cinnamon-colored eyes, was more than skin-deep.

And they whispered he was different.

Reno enjoyed being a loner for good reason. He came from a medicine family of shape-shifters. But even this secret power had not protected him—or his family. His wife, Ilona, and his three-year-old daughter, Sarah, were dead. Murdered by Army General Hampton in their former home on USMC base in Camp Pendleton, California. Bitterness thrummed through Reno as he savagely pushed the toe of his scarred leather boot against several smaller pieces of gray granite that were in his way.

The sun beat down upon Manchahi's naked shoulders, grown dark red over time, shouting his half-Apache heritage. With his straight black hair grazing his thick shoulders, copper skin and broad face with high cheekbones, everyone knew he was Indian. When he'd first arrived at the brig, some of the prisoners taunted him and called him Geronimo. Something strange happened to Reno during his fight with the name-calling prisoners. Leaning down after he'd won the scuffle, he'd snarled into each of their bloodied faces that if they were going to call him anything, they would call him *gan,* which was the Apache word for *devil.*

His attackers had been shocked by the wounds on their faces, the deep claw marks. Reno recalled doubling his fist as they'd attacked him en masse. In that split second, he'd gone into an altered state of consciousness. In times of danger, he transformed into a jaguar. A deep, growling sound had emitted from his throat as he defended himself in the three-against-one fracas. It all happened so fast that he thought he had imagined it. He'd seen his hands morph into a forearm and paw, claws extended. The slashes left on the three men's faces after the fight told him he'd begun to shape-shift. A fist made bruises and swelling, not four perfect, deep claw marks. Stunned and anxious, he hid the knowledge of what else he was from these prisoners. Reno's only defense was to make all the prisoners so damned scared of him and remain a loner.

Alone. Yeah, he was alone, all right. The steel hammer swept downward with hellish ferocity. As the granite groaned in protest, Reno shut his eyes for just a moment. Sweat dripped off his nose and square chin.

Straightening, he wiped his furrowed, wet brow and looked into the pale blue sky. What got his attention was the startling cry of a red-tailed hawk as it flew over the brig yard.

Squinting, he watched the bird. Reno could make out the rust-colored tail on the hawk. As a kid growing up on the Apache reservation in Arizona, Reno knew that all animals that appeared before him were messengers.

Brother, what message do you bring me? Reno knew one had to ask in order to receive. Allowing the sledgehammer to drop to his side, he concentrated on the hawk who wheeled in tightening circles above him.

Freedom! the hawk cried in return.

Reno shook his head, his black hair moving against his broad, thickset shoulders. *Freedom? No way, Brother. No way.* Figuring that he was making up the hawk's shrill message, Reno turned away. Back to his rocks. Back to picturing Hampton's smug face.

Freedom!

* * * * *

*Look for UNFORGIVEN by Lindsay McKenna,
the spine-tingling launch title from
Silhouette Nocturne™.
Available September 26, wherever books
are sold.*

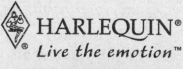

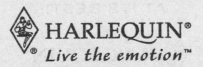

HARLEQUIN®
INTRIGUE®

WE'LL LEAVE YOU BREATHLESS!

If you've been looking for thrilling tales of contemporary passion and sensuous love stories with taut, edge-of-the-seat suspense—then you'll love Harlequin Intrigue!

Every month, you'll meet six new heroes who are guaranteed to make your spine tingle and your pulse pound. With them you'll enter into the exciting world of Harlequin Intrigue— where your life is on the line and so is your heart!

THAT'S INTRIGUE— ROMANTIC SUSPENSE AT ITS BEST!

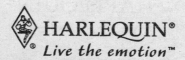

HARLEQUIN®
Live the emotion™